Eric Ambler was born into a fami[ly ...]
years helped out as a puppetee[r ...]
engineering as a full time career, alt[hough this] quickly gave way to writing. In World War II he entered the army and looked likely to fight in the line, but was soon after commissioned and ended the war as assistant director of the army film unit and a Lieutenant-Colonel.

This experience translated into civilian life and Ambler had a very successful career as a screen writer, receiving an Academy Award for his work on *The Cruel Sea* by Nicolas Monsarrat in 1953. Many of his own works have been filmed, the most famous probably being *Light of Day*, filmed as *Topkapi* under which title it is now published.

He established a reputation as a thriller writer of extraordinary depth and originality and received many other accolades during his lifetime, including two *Edgar Awards* from *The Mystery Writers of America* (best novel for *Topkapi* and best biographical work for *Here Lies Eric Ambler)*, and two *Gold Dagger Awards* from the *Crime Writer's Association (Passage of Arms* and *The Levanter)*.

Often credited as being the inventor of the modern political thriller, John Le Carre once described Ambler as '*the source on which we all draw.*' A recurring theme in his works is the success of the well meaning yet somewhat bungling amateur who triumphs in the face of both adversity and hardened professionals.

Ambler wrote under his own name and also during the 1950's a series of novels as *Eliot Reed*, with *Charles Rhodda*. These are now published under the '*Ambler*' umbrella.

Works of **ERIC AMBLER** published by **HOUSE OF STRATUS**

DOCTOR FRIGO
JUDGMENT ON DELTCHEV
THE LEVANTER
THE SCHIRMER INHERITANCE
THE SIEGE OF THE VILLA LIPP (Also as 'Send No More Roses')
TOPKAPI (Also as 'The Light Of Day')

Originally as Eliot Reed with Charles Rhodda:
CHARTER TO DANGER
THE MARAS AFFAIR
PASSPORT TO PANIC
TENDER TO DANGER (Also as 'Tender To Moonlight')
SKYTIP

Autobiography:
HERE LIES ERIC AMBLER

Skytip

eric Ambler

(Writing as Eliot Reed with Charles Rhodda)

Copyright © Eric Ambler 1951; House of Stratus 2010

All rights reserved. No part of this publication may be reproduced, stored in a retrieval system, or transmitted, in any form, or by any means (electronic, mechanical, photocopying, recording, or otherwise), without the prior permission of the publisher. Any person who does any unauthorised act in relation to this publication may be liable to criminal prosecution and civil claims for damages.

The right of Eric Ambler to be identified as the author of this work has been asserted.

This edition published in 2009 by House of Stratus, an imprint of Stratus Books Ltd., Lisandra House, Fore Street, Looe, Cornwall, PL13 1AD, U.K.

www.houseofstratus.com

Typeset, printed and bound by House of Stratus.

A catalogue record for this book is available from the British Library and the Library of Congress.

ISBN 0-7551-2379-4
EAN 978-0-7551-2379-7

This book is sold subject to the condition that it shall not be lent, resold, hired out, or otherwise circulated without the publisher's express prior consent in any form of binding, or cover, other than the original as herein published and without a similar condition being imposed on any subsequent purchaser, or bona fide possessor.

This is a fictional work and all characters are drawn from the author's imagination. Any resemblance or similarities to persons either living or dead are entirely coincidental.

Chapter 1

SOMETIMES, chance operates with a dreadful sort of humour that seems to spring from the workings of a diseased controlling mind.

One man happens to cut a piece of wet blind-cord and a whole political movement totters. This same man lends another the price of a train fare to London and as a consequence is himself sent by rail to his death. A man is murdered because he will not reveal a secret and also because he will. A girl allies herself to a traitor and destroys him by forgetting that, without a key, you cannot open a spring lock.

At least, that was how it all seemed. The story even began grotesquely, with a wry joke.

"Rest", said the doctor, "complete rest and no excitement. Go to Scotland or Cornwall, right away from everything to do with London and your work."

That was the joke. Fortunately, the patient did not see it.

He pressed his lips together irritably. "I'm afraid I've far too much work to do. There's nothing the matter with me that a few sleeping-pills won't put right. Perhaps later in the year. . ."

"After the breakdown?" inquired the doctor pleasantly. "Yes, you could go then I suppose. But you'll have to spend six months away in that case instead of two. Would you mind that?"

"Can we dispense with the pawky wit?"

"Certainly. On second thoughts you'd better make it Cornwall. About the bad nights, I'll give you something for them; but the real need for the moment is rest, fresh air and quiet."

"You don't seem to understand. I simply cannot afford the time."

"I know. That's the trouble with you bankrupts."

"I assure you . . ."

"Of course you do." The doctor's pale smile had no more than a hint of weariness in it. "It was emotional insolvency I was talking about. Sometimes the bills pile up for years and it seems not to matter. Then, something happens and they're all presented for payment at once."

"Something? What something?"

The doctor looked at his patient's tie. "Something like letting your wife divorce you."

"That means nothing to me now."

"No?"

Peter Ackland was silent. The doctor was a friend of his, but at that moment he disliked the pompous ass intensely, and had a desperate desire to prove him wrong.

He said lamely: "I fail to see what my divorce has to do with it. It was a very good thing. You said so yourself."

The doctor nodded vaguely. "Something happens," he repeated. "The tensions rise. Then comes the crack-up. It may disguise itself as a peptic ulcer or heart trouble or alcoholism, but the effect is the same – Peter Ackland, the brilliant young architect, becomes something less than he might have been. Early promise is unfulfilled. The accounts are squared."

"I'm neither brilliant nor very young. But at the present moment I feel well on the way to becoming an alcoholic."

"Whisky and soda?"

"Thanks."

The doctor went to the decanter and poured two drinks. "You're lucky," he said. "Your trouble is more thinly disguised – insomnia, depression, an anxiety state revealed as irritability – it shows itself for what it is, an emotional sickness."

"For which the cure is a few weeks in Cornwall. I know."

The doctor handed him a drink. "Not the cure, Peter. Merely a necessary relief for the body and a chance for the mind to work out its own salvation. Cheers."

Peter looked at his drink, then shrugged. "Cheers," he said.

Later, he had a second drink.

The doctor had known just the place, of course; Trevone Farm near Bosverran; delightful people, wonderful food, Cornish cream, fresh eggs. He would write and arrange everything.

"Can you leave next week? You don't have to worry about anything. Cornish Riviera from Paddington. Get out at Par. Take the local from there to Bosverran Road. Tregethney will meet you with his truck. The farm's quite a way from the station, really quiet and peaceful."

As the Cornish Riviera express rushed him westward some days later, Peter was a little conscience-stricken over his churlishness. Even with the protracted weariness of the main journey and its depressing aftermath, the discomfort of the spur line train, this mild contrition persisted. Then he got to Bosverran Road and there was no Tregethney, no truck, and no more daylight, only an elderly porter, a canopy rain-shelter, and a single strip of platform that stretched out sadly in the dusk like the pathway to a tomb.

After half an hour there was still no truck. The porter became curious. When he heard the name of the stranded traveller, he brought out some bad news, Sam Tregethney had collected the advance luggage that morning. He wasn't expecting a guest till tomorrow.

"Ridiculous! He was clearly informed. . . ."

Peter checked himself. "Clearly" was evidently not the word.

"My dear life!" the porter said. "It's a long walk to Trevone Farm."

The Tregethneys were not on the 'phone. If Mr. Ackland wanted to hire a car, he might find one at the petrol pump a little distance along the road.

That little distance was well over a mile. There was a petrol pump all right, but it was closed down for the night, and the tin shed behind it was bolted and padlocked.

This was too much. For a moment he stared at the padlock in blank dismay. Then despair gave way to irritation and irritation grew into anger. The doctor had deliberately done this to him, cast him out into the night of this forlorn, padlocked country to punish him. They were all in collusion – doctor, porter, the hypothetical Tregethney. The deserted road ran between the bleak fields to nowhere. All right! He would immediately go back to London. He would go to the doctor's house at dead of night and he would hammer . . .

He pulled himself up sharply. If he went on like this the empty road would lead to paranoia. He had certainly a right to be irritated, but he mustn't make too much of it.

He went on, walking, because there no longer seemed to be any point in going back. The light valise he carried was beginning to feel as if someone had slipped a pig of lead into it, when he came to a cottage and stopped. The occupants could give him no hope of a car, but if he hurried to the cross-roads, he would be in time to catch the bus to Bosverran town.

Comforted by the assurance that people really lived in the land, he hurried. He saw the bus coming through the dusk, and had to run for it. The bus ripped off another mile, heading into the darkening west towards the saw-toothed skyline of the china clay country, racing nearer and nearer, till the great white skytips of rubble grew monstrous, looking in the darkness like snow peaks.

Bosverran was a small town, rather dimly lighted. As the bus plunged into it, Peter made out a sprawl of houses around a short shopping street with a square-towered church at one end and a gabled chapel at the other. When he got down at the post-office, he looked for a pub. He was tired, hungry, thirsty, and needed information. He pushed open the first door that promised him succour.

Trade was not brisk. There were a couple of customers with a pint apiece in the tap-room and some noise of dart-players from an adjoining parlour. The customers looked up from their beer to study him suspiciously. All he could see behind the bar was a large tabby cat sitting straight up in an office-chair with a leather cushion. The cat, narrow-eyed, seemed to regard him with even more suspicion than the customers. Peter was embarrassed. He was aware of an insane desire to address the cat rather than wait for somebody to come.

A little man came, dark, with a skin like old vellum stretched tightly over the bones of a wedge-shaped countenance. In a way he looked something like the cat, except that he had a deep Celtic gloom in his eyes and his general air was one of excessive solemnity. The cat was merely suspicious.

Peter bought beer and sandwiches, then asked where he could get accommodation for the night.

The landlord shook his head. "I don't know," he said. "We can't do nothing here. They might put you up at the Commercial but I did hear they was full up. You from London, likely?"

"Yes."

"All the way from London without a room to go to?"

The cat rose on its chair and clawed the edge of the bar to get a closer look at this improvident traveller. Peter explained his situation.

"Trevone Farm," the landlord said. "That's just along the road. You can walk it in a few minutes."

"Perhaps I could get a car?"

"Take your paws off the counter, Douglas!" the landlord admonished the cat. "Haven't I told you it's bad manners."

Douglas got down coolly.

It seemed that all the cars – there were not so many – had taken people over to a dance at Liskeard. But there was no need for a car. All you had to do was take the eastward road, bear to the left at the big skytip, and carry on. There was only one farm along the lane; impossible to mistake it.

"Likely you'd better wait for the moon," the landlord added. "It'll be rising before long."

Peter sighed inwardly. "Give me another bitter, and have a drink yourself."

"Never touch the stuff," the landlord complained. "It just turns my stomach. I got a cup of tea coming up. You want some more sandwiches, I'll get the missus to cut them."

At the end of an hour Peter was trudging again, climbing the hill towards the skytip. On the rise he looked out over the country, seeing the full sweep of the distorted landscape for the first time. The great white rubble dumps were like the carcases of lunar volcanoes, taking the moon's light, as the moon took that of the sun, to give an illusion

5

of radiance.

He switched hands on the valise, and walked on up the road.

Now the nearer tip seemed to bar his way, sprawling wide and rearing high above him. Then the road forked, one branch winding off to the right into the clay country, the other curving round the base of the great mound in front of him. He remembered the landlord's injunction to bear to the left, and, as he came round the bend, he saw a lighted window near at hand.

If there was only one farm, this must be it.

He went forward. Across the road from the skytip the house took shape, a cottage type of building, two-storeyed, with a high-pitched roof. He had climbed steadily from the town to this point. Now the road ahead dipped down again and deteriorated into a cart-track or lane, with ragged, overgrown walls.

Peter examined the house. It might be a farm, but the absence of the usual outbuildings made him doubtful. All the same, he could see nothing else in the neighbourhood, and he wasn't going to go on without an inquiry.

The light came from an upstairs room. The ground floor was in darkness. Peter found a door and struck a match to look for a bell-push. There was no bell, only an old iron knocker, and the impression it made was not good. It was too large for the door, and it was hung crookedly.

Peter scowled, and was still scowling when the match burned him. The number of badly hung knockers....

This one, nevertheless, could produce a good healthy bang, even for a critical architect. Bang, bang, bang!

Nothing happened. No sound in the house. After nearly a minute, he knocked again, and stepped back from the porch to gaze up at the lighted window. He thought of giving a hail, but, before he could open his mouth, the light was switched off. He waited, returning to the porch. He heard what sounded like a cautious step. He looked for at least a gleam from the ground floor, but the darkness was unbroken, and a long silence followed the shuffling step. Then a voice spoke from behind the door.

"Who's there? What do you want?"

"Is this Trevone Farm?"

"No, it isn't. Who are you?"

The voice had a dead, flat sound, but the words, the questioning, carried a suggestion of anxiety to Peter.

"I'm sorry," he said. "I'm looking for Trevone Farm, They were supposed to meet me at the station, but there seems to have been some hitch."

At last a glimmer from the bottom of the door showed that a light had been turned on. Sounds followed. Bolts were pulled back, a key was turned, and Peter faced the bulb of a torch. He could see that the door, open a few inches, was held by a chain. He could see nothing else; the torch was a glaring shield for the man behind it.

Peter made a conscious effort to quell a new resentment.

"I hope I haven't disturbed you," he said. "I'm quite a stranger in the neighbourhood."

"Wait!"

The door was closed, the chain clinked, the door was opened again. Now there was no torch; the light of a pendent bulb revealed fully a man in a tweed jacket arid grey flannel slacks.

He was tall and round-shouldered with a small round paunch like a child's. He must have been in the late forties; a pink, worried-looking man with a fair, close-clipped moustache. His right hand was holding something in the pocket of his jacket, but it wasn't the torch. He had put that down on a table near the door.

"The farm's half a mile down the lane. This is Trevone Cottage. Sorry to be slow answering. Callers are rare in these parts."

The voice came to life a little with the wish to be affable. The right hand came from the jacket pocket to underline the affability with a gesture. The jacket sagged as if there were something weighty in that pocket, but Peter noticed the fact without paying it attention. He was interested in the man's eyes. They were pale, faded and slightly vacuous, yet their expression held anxiety, relief, eagerness and misery all at the same time. It was odd.

At the first moment of the encounter there had been great fear in them. Still, as he had said, callers were rare; a nervous man might well be scared at night by a knock at the door.

"Down from London, eh?" he was saying.

"Yes." Peter nodded. "Just for a rest."

"I live here most of the time. The name's Braddock."

"Mine's Ackland."

"Ah, yes, of course. I heard you were coming." The relief was more apparent now. "Architect or something, aren't you? Everything gets around down here, unless you're very cautious. I rent this place from the Tregethneys, so I can't escape the farm gossip. Let me know if there's anything I can do for you. I'm a Londoner myself."

"Thanks. You're very kind."

"We're next door neighbours, you know."

He came out on to the porch holding his arms slightly in front of him, and Peter marked that singular trick for the first time. It was for all the world as if the man were trying to squeeze through a narrow gap in a hedge.

"I'd walk along the lane with you," he said, "only I'm rather busy, and you can't possibly miss the farm. It's on the right. The first white gate you come to. You'll see it quite clearly in this moon."

And that was all of Henry Braddock for the time being.

The first white gate opened the way to a household that immediately became afluster with apologies, explanations, and the hasty preparation of a meal. The doctor's letter was produced, and there, sure enough, was tomorrow's date. Nevertheless, the two Tregethneys beat their breasts and lamented loudly that a guest of theirs should have been left to wander through the wilderness in search of their house. A wonder it was that Mr. Ackland had found it! A miracle!

Mr. Ackland said the error was of no consequence. He begged his hosts not to inconvenience themselves, but nothing would stay their activity. The farmhouse was neat and clean and bright with light, and open to the night. It was in agreeable contrast to that dour, lock-guarded place behind the great skytip at the top of the lane. And now, in these domestic surroundings, it seemed to Peter that the man

Braddock was a peculiar person – at least odd. One must be careful not to exaggerate.

He brought up the subject as soon as the Tregethneys gave him an opportunity.

"I saw your tenant up the lane. He directed me here."

"Mr. Braddock?" The farmer gave a mildly questioning inflection to the name. Obviously it meant nothing sinister to him.

"Does he live there all alone?"

"His wife's dead," Mrs. Tregethney answered. "Killed in the blitz. In Liverpool. Mr. Braddock's a nice gentleman and a good tenant. If he likes to live alone, I suppose he can please himself."

"He's been with us since two years or more," Tregethney added quickly, and Peter knew that Mr. Braddock was not liked.

"Retired, I suppose?"

"In a way of speaking, perhaps. He's a writer. He writes books."

"I see. That explains it. He likes peace and quiet."

"I wouldn't know about that," Tregethney said. "He does keep himself to himself in his house. Except the woman who goes there to clean, you never see anyone at the place. Otherwise he's friendly. No airs about him," he persisted doggedly. "Always ready to buy a drink."

"We see a good bit of him," Mrs. Tregethney volunteered. "He comes here for his milk. You'll see a lot of him yourself, no doubt. He's a learned man, and travelled. You and him'll have a lot in common."

Peter quailed.

Tregethney came from a shelf with a blue-bound volume in his hand.

"He gave us one of his books when he first came here. Wrote in it, too. If you look in the front, you'll see what he wrote."

Peter took the book and looked at the title: *Yugoslavia Tomorrow – A Study in Politics* – By George Coke.

He turned to the autograph. "To Paul and Ruth Tregethney, with the compliments of George Coke and the undying gratitude of Henry Braddock."

The letters were self-consciously well formed. It was the writing of a persevering schoolboy.

Mrs. Tregethney said: "If you ask me, I don't think he ever got over his wife's death."

To Peter the words were a rather startling *non sequitur*. He had to come back from a distance to grasp them.

"I'd like to read it," he said lamely.

"That's right," Tregethney agreed. "There's a lot in it. Surprising what a man thinks of to print in a book. Of course, it's all about this Yugoslav place before the war. Things have changed, I dare say. And Mr. Braddock, he's changed, too, I imagine. He don't get about so much as he did. Up to London now and then's about as far as he goes."

Peter took the book to bed with him, but read only a little of it. The skittish journalese, the faded jargon, the solemn air of authority irritated him. But, in another way, they also amused him. The knowing self-important traveller was so unlike the Braddock he had seen, the spinsterish Braddock who bolted and chained his doors against the night. And what was it, by the way, that had made the man's jacket sag when he took his hand from the pocket?

It might have been anything. It might have been a revolver.

A less amusing series of ideas began to flow through Peter Ackland's mind. Why should he suddenly be evolving melodramatic fantasies about a harmless creature with whom he had had a few moments conversation on a doorstep? Revolver? Fiddlesticks! Most likely a pair of pliers or a spanner. Probably he had been changing the washer on a tap, or mending a fuse. Either of those things, too, would account for the delay in answering the door. Peter began to sweat. A wave of depression came. The abysmal absurdities of which his mind was capable appalled him. "Hovering on the edge of a nervous breakdown." The phrase came echoing back to him from the pages of a dozen novels. But now it seemed to have acquired a peculiar force. Hovering? That was to put it mildly. It was time he pulled himself together. In future he would take precautions.

He would defeat the enemy. He would take his sleeping-pills an hour earlier and so deprive these half-waking fantasies of their opportunities. He would take long exhausting walks. He would inhale fresh air. He would gossip with the Tregethneys in their kitchen. He would read the Bible from cover to cover. He would....

His mind wandered on and he slept. But in one part of it he knew that he had not disposed of the problem of Braddock, and the fact troubled him. It kept on troubling him. That night and afterwards.

Chapter 2

MANY ages ago when the earth began to cool, a thin crust of rock formed upon its surface. Soon, the condensation of water vapour was possible, oceans came into being and another process began; the laying down of new rock strata – the limestones, shales and sands – formed from the water-eroded sediments of earlier rocks. But, while on the surface the new was evolved, beneath, all was still molten and, as the crust deepened and contracted, the tensions within became greater. Here, under the huge pressures and temperatures to which they were being subjected, the primordial stuffs of the planet changed into quartz, mica, sphene, garnet, hornblende, apatite, biotite, zircon and felspar; and these, the constituents of granite, were intermingled in vast convulsive masses, separated from the basalt layers but no less volcanic. It was the gigantic eruptions and surgings of these masses which eventually threw up the land continents of the world and the great igneous rock systems that pierce the stratified surface of it.

As the granite outcrops cooled, however, further changes often took place in their composition. In some regions, for instance, the granite began to rot; certain acid vapours which had erupted with it caused the felspar to decompose.

Millions of years later in China from a hill, Kao-ling, men extracted some of this decomposed felspar and found a use for it. In the early part of the eighteenth century a French missionary sent specimens of the stuff to Europe. He called it "kaolin", and it was, he said, the essential ingredients of the famous Chinese porcelains. Soon afterwards, a Plymouth man found the great kaolin deposits of Cornwall and out of this discovery of the Cornish "china-clay" a new industry evolved. Men learned that with jets of water they could wash the kaolin out of the crevices between the other constituents of the old rock and collect it by precipitation. The useless granitic remains they left to accumulate by the clay pits. With the years these accumulations grew until the landscape of the clay country became encrusted with white conical heaps hundreds of feet high; and, from the floor of each pit, rail-tracks ran up to ground level and thence on up the steep side of the rising heap, bearing steel-bellied wagons to discharge their loads of waste at the summit.

They called these heaps skytips.

Peter liked them; at first, that is. He wandered among them and came to know them. When he looked out of his bedroom window in the mornings, he found the landscape delightfully spectacular. There was a bland other-worldliness about it that appealed to him. Later he would discover that by moonlight it could be as stark as a bleached bone and that in the wreathing sea-mist it had a spectral impermanence that was not agreeable; but for the first few days there was nothing but sunshine, and, when there was a stiff breeze blowing, white dust would spurt from the tips and they would seem to him like snow-plumed mountain peaks. He found them soothing.

It was several days before Peter saw Braddock again. Twice he heard him. On alternate days Braddock came to get milk, and Peter's deck-chair in the small farmhouse garden was within earshot of the side door; but the sound of the writer's voice was enough. Certainly, Peter was feeling better; but he guessed warily that the improvement was far from real and that five minutes of Henry Braddock would shatter his fragile illusion of well-being very quickly. As it was, the man's tone of voice alone conjured up uncomfortable memories of a moment of hysteria he wished to forget. He had taken his walks in directions that avoided Braddock's house.

But avoiding Braddock also meant avoiding Bosverran, for the only reasonable road into the town from Trevone Farm passed by the house; and to avoid Bosverran indefinitely was to be seriously inconvenienced. The post-office, the tobacconist, and the circulating library were all in the town. So were the pubs. But it was Mrs. Tregethney who actually sealed Peter's fate. She wanted his emergency ration card and the local Food Office was in Bosverran. On the fifth morning of his stay there he set off up the lane down which he had stumbled five nights before.

He saw Braddock long before he came to the house. He was in the front garden staring up aimlessly at the big skytip that overshadowed it. It was almost as if the man was waiting for him. Then Braddock turned and waved and Peter knew that he had in fact been awaited. From an upstairs room of the house Braddock must have seen him approaching.

Peter walked on gloomily. He did not wave back. For a minute or so he would pretend that he did not recognise Braddock. Indeed, why should he? As he walked on he looked out over the country that went dancing down to the blue Cornish sea. He looked over field and croft and wasteland, over a tilted plane of green scored by the hard lines of stone walls. But his eyes kept being drawn back to the skytip that obscured the southward view. It seemed to lean towards the house as if about to engulf it, but that of course was an optical illusion. The base of the tip was at least two hundred yards away from the garden gate.

His professional interest faintly aroused, Peter took for a measuring rod the Nelson column. The cone out-topped the Admiral by well over a hundred feet; and, dumped down in Trafalgar Square, it would have buried not merely the lions, but the fountains as well, and reached perhaps to the top of Whitehall. Perhaps . . .

"Hullo there! Remember me?"

Braddock was a few yards away, looking at him with an anxious grin. Peter suffered a twinge of remorse for his churlishness. Braddock reminded him irresistibly of a decrepit Airedale, wagging his tail, but still uncertain whether he would be cursed or patted.

Peter affected a start of recognition. "Oh yes, of course. How do you do?"

"I hear you got settled in all right. Going into town?"

"Yes." Where else could he be going?

"I'm going in myself. Want to get a bit of fish before it's all sold. I'll walk down with you if you don't mind waiting a jiff."

"Fine."

A jiff!

"Just going to water the horse," said Braddock and plunged into the house.

Peter stared at the place. Night had been merciful. It was a monster; vilely planned, if planned at all, built all askew, as if anything to hand had been used in its construction; small windows placed without any consideration for a formal pattern, or for utility; glazing bars too fat, much too fat; some mellowness in the old stone walls, but marred by hideous pointing with white lime; and right over the approach to the door there was an overflow pipe. That pipe really was an offence. It projected from the wall a few feet below the sloping roof above the entrance. At some time or other there had been a leak, and the wind had blown the water against the wall. There was an ugly plume of green lichen on the wall to mark the occasion. The builder who had put that pipe there should starve.

Braddock bustled out, slamming the front door behind him.

"All present and correct," he said.

They walked down the road towards the town. Braddock talked about the fishmonger and the grocer. There was at first a kind of desperate affability about him, as if he were making an effort he knew to be unavailing to gain a friend. But before they had gone far, his spate of gaiety was spent, dying in an unresolved cadence. Peter had to take up the burden of making talk.

"I've been reading one of your books," he said.

"Which one?" The voice was carefully indifferent.

"*Yugoslavia Tomorrow.*"

"Oh, that one! I remember. What did you think of it?"

"Well, I only took a glance at it. I see you've published quite a lot."

"A dozen or so. One has to live."

"Any novels?"

"No. All non-fiction. Travelled a bit in my day, you know: France, Germany, Italy, the Balkans." Braddock rallied a little in spirit. "Used to do articles for some of the slicks and the motor journals. You know the stuff – 'Through the Balkans with a Straight Eight.' Not a bad racket, really. The car people used to pay all expenses, for the sake of the publicity. Then I'd rehash the stuff and cook up a travel book. *Yugoslavia Tomorrow* was one I did like that. Published a month before the war."

"Very interesting."

"Interesting?" Braddock looked dubious. "It pulled the shekels in all right. But I made my mark as a political writer, really."

"Oh? I'm afraid I haven't kept in close touch." Peter felt that something was due to the self-esteem of the author.

Braddock seemed not to hear. "Yes," he went on, "I've done several political books. *A Study in Terrorism* by Charles Lebrun. That was mine. Sold ten thousand copies at twelve and six. You may have read it."

"I think I missed it. Do you always use pen-names?"

"Why not?" He grinned cunningly. "Pick the name to suit the matter. That's my rule. When it comes to European politics, the public likes a foreign name. Makes them feel they're getting inside information. I'll have to see if I can find a copy of *Study in Terrorism* for you. It's all about the rise of the Nazis, from the Gestapo angle."

Peter felt that something else was due. "There've been quite a lot of books about the rise of the Nazis, haven't there?"

"Naturally. It was pay-dirt while it lasted. Every little scribbler was running round the Continent chasing after it, but I got the best stuff of the lot in mine. Ten thousand copies! It ought to have sold a hundred thousand. Then some people might have understood what was brewing. I had some sources of information in those days. The book sounds a bit pre-war, I suppose, but it's not so dated, considering what's going on in Europe this very minute. All the shooting didn't settle a thing."

Peter began to consider means of escape. They were approaching the town.

"With your sources of information," he said, "you must have been a useful man while the shooting was on."

"You'd have thought so, wouldn't you?" Braddock slumped back into the darker mood. "I was right at the front door, with bells on, ready for the best intelligence job they could hand out." He shook his head bitterly. "Not on your life, old chap! I applied three times. Turned down flat each time. And do you know why?"

"Why?"

"Languages," Braddock said contemptuously. "In the end I managed to get an interview – not with a responsible officer. Oh, no! Some little pipsqueak of a major with glasses. Asked me to translate a ream of German technical stuff, if you please. I told him if he wanted that sort of thing, he'd come to the wrong shop. Do you blame me? Anyone can learn a language if he has the time to spare, but it's not everyone knows his way around like I do."

Peter didn't know what to say. He said nothing.

"So they kept me cooped up in the Pay Corps when I might have been out on a job of real importance."

"Too bad."

"Well, I got my chance in the end. When Amgot came along, I was right in on the ground floor. I had a good job in the Ruhr for a time. Then they wanted to ship me to the East. I said 'No thank you', and we parted company."

"You must have managed to get hold of some good copy."

"Well, I'm always getting hold of something. It's a useful thing when you've got sources of information."

"You're working on a new book, I suppose? What's it about this time? Politics? Germany?"

Braddock halted, and looked morosely back over the clay country. Peter waited for an answer, but did not get it.

"It's outrageous," Braddock said, "the way they've ruined the landscape with those refuse dumps."

The evasion was so naive that Peter realised that his question had touched a sensitive spot. Braddock's pink face had gone a deeper pink. But why? Perhaps the book was not coming along too well. Perhaps, among the writers of Braddock's world, it was tactless to ask about work in progress, as tactless as asking a professional thief about his plans for the future.

"Outrageous!" Braddock repeated with emphasis. "Dumps of rubble, as far as you can see. They destroy the whole scene."

Peter had to accept the change of subject. He looked at the saw-tooth skyline of the tips. "They make a scene in themselves. They're not without an effect." The word "unearthly" came to him, but he rejected it. "Dramatic," he added, feeling that his statement needed strengthening.

"Mountains of the moon. That sort of thing." Braddock sneered. "I call it vandalism, mutilation, outrage. You take a look at the pits they've dug all round this place. Think of the beauty they've destroyed."

"I doubt if there was much beauty here before they started digging. It's pretty bleak, most of it."

"Well, they get on your nerves, those damned skytips. Live among them long enough, and you begin to dream about them. They're all exactly alike, as if they've been turned out of a mould."

Peter stared at Braddock wondering about him as they walked on down the lane. Braddock picked his way carefully over a rough patch. He was slightly pigeon-toed and his feet were too small for his height. They made him seem unstable.

"There's something sinister about them," he said.

Peter did not reply. For, suddenly, he had the impression that Braddock was no longer talking of skytips, but of something, or someone else; and clearly that was absurd. Quite clearly. He dismissed the thought firmly.

"Where's the Food Office?" he asked.

The little town gave an impression of bustling self-importance during the morning shopping hour. It was an out-of-the-way place, neglected by guide-books and unknown to the crowds who thronged the big holiday resorts; but visitors came in season – people who could not get accommodation elsewhere, or people who liked quiet and sought the remote farms that fringed the clay country.

Bosverran's self-importance derived not from the fact that it was a small , but from the feeling that it was a very large village. The strutted up and down the short High Street with their arrier bags and who made a gossip forum in every shop but urban in character. Strangers must stand out from apart if not conspicuously different.

Peter was coming from the Food Office in the Town Hall, when he saw the girl, and she was certainly conspicuously different.

Braddock, mercifully, had gone off by himself in search of fish, and Peter was to meet him at the Memorial for the journey back. Unsure of the way, he stood for a moment on the steps of the Town Hall to get his bearings. She was hesitating in a similar fashion outside the post office on the opposite side of the street.

She was dark, chic, and very lovely, but he noted these things as he might note that the sun was shining. His wife had been chic and very lovely, too. There was something else about this girl. But what?

She looked up and down the street, frowning. She glanced at the post office clock and pressed her lips together. Person, car, whatever should have been there, was not there. After a moment or two she decided not to wait and walked away across the street.

It was not until she had disappeared that Peter realised what the something was about her. He had seen her before, somewhere. But when?

Puzzled and vaguely irritated he walked in the direction of the Memorial. That was the direction the girl had taken, but he did not see her on the way.

"Got a nice bit of hake," said Braddock briskly as he arrived.

"Good."

"What about a snifter at the *Green Dragon*?"

"Where's that?"

"Just up the road there." Braddock flourished his limp parcel like a sword in the direction of the High Street, and they set off.

"There's nothing like a nice bit of hake, I always say." Braddock eyed Peter facetiously. "What do *you* always **say**?"

"Nothing like it," said Peter.

Then he saw the girl again, and, at the same moment, out of the corner of his eye, he saw Braddock's grin vanish.

She was coming toward him, still with that slightly nettled air of searching for someone who shouldn't be lost.

She passed within a foot of him, and once more he had the feeling of having seen her before. She walked easily and comfortably in a good tweed suit with a shape to it. He caught the faintest breath of scent as she passed. She looked self-assured and very competent.

"Nothing like it," he repeated feebly and then realised that Braddock was no longer beside him. He looked round, startled. The man had disappeared. Then Peter saw him in a newsagent's shop, buying a paper.

The girl was more interesting. Just by the Memorial she had stopped and was signalling to someone.

A large cream-coloured car, negotiating the corner, swung round and pulled into the kerb beside her. She said something sharply to the chauffeur. He began to explain and apologise. She listened for a moment impatiently, then, before he could get out to open the door for her, she stepped into the back seat. The door slammed. The chauffeur knitted his brow. The car moved off.

With a fluid, oily purr it filtered through the mixed traffic in the High Street. Peter watched it, more than ever curious about its passenger, and, as it approached him, he saw what looked like some heraldic emblem on its door. It passed close to him, and he had no difficulty in observing the emblem: a hand holding a sword, and under it the letters, N.L.P.

The sword was *Excalibur*. The letters stood for the National League of Patriots, the new political movement, the party with a cure for every ill.

Braddock came from the newsagent's with a paper under his arm.

"Now for that drink," he said.

Peter had a sense of anticlimax. In a gleam from *Excalibur* the mystery of the girl was exposed. He had seen her on the platform at a political meeting, attendant on the orator of the evening. She was, no doubt, some sort of secretary.

That was the trouble with people. In architecture you could tell the Doric from the Ionic at a glance, and you were unlikely ever to confuse the Low Dutch with the early Tudor when it came to gables. With people it was so much more difficult. English Perpendicular, you thought, and it turned out to be Political Baroque.

He shrugged mentally and turned to Braddock. He said: "Why

didn't you want to meet that girl?"

"I don't understand." Braddock was a poor actor.

"The dark girl," he persisted. "The minute you saw her you ducked into that shop."

"Ducked? My dear chap, I don't know what you're talking about. I never saw any girl, dark, fair, or medium. I went into the shop to get a paper. I suddenly remembered."

He flourished his purchase, exhibiting the front page, and once more Peter was confronted by the symbol of *Excalibur*, the sword held aloft by a hand emerging from deep waters.

The paper was the weekly organ of the N.L.P.

The *Green Dragon* proved to be the public house with the dyspeptic landlord and the cat named Douglas at which Peter had called on the night of his arrival. But it was a while before he noticed the fact. He entered the bar in some confusion. He was in a state of what he was now beginning to recognise and label as "Braddock jitters". He looked at the unwitting cause with something like hatred in his heart.

Braddock was at his breeziest in a pub. He waved greetings, exchanged local jokes with the other customers, and was facetiously gallant to the landlord's wife. He drank a Dutch gin, washed it down with bottled beer, and vanished in the direction of the darts room.

He had flung the paper he had bought on to the corner window ledge with his hat and his hake. Peter picked up the paper and looked at it.

The *Round Table* was a propaganda sheet for that curious movement, the National League of Patriots. On one side of the title block was an illustration of *Excalibur* and on the other a representation of the Holy Grail standing in a beam of somewhat dusty sunshine. The League's appropriation of the Arthurian myth was affirmed by a note in miniscule type under each drawing to the effect that the designs were copyright by the N.L.P.

Inside, the paper reported meetings and collections up and down the country, and it carried an article explaining why the movement was "making giant strides". There was another article condemning all other parties and movements, and it was particularly bitter about a

"Government that permitted the re-emergence of the Fascist-Nazi adder in England's green and pleasant land." There was but one true movement for Patriots, and its Prophet was Arthur Lamorak-Britt, M.P., whose handsome, heavy face with the grave, searching eyes confronted you on page one in a fine job of half-tone engraving.

If you wanted an actor for an Arthurian pageant, Mr. Britt was certainly the man for the part. The camera, doubtless with the assistance of a competent re-toucher, made him a composite of every knight that ever came to Camelot. On the platform, in the round, he had not given Peter the same impression of spirituality. Perhaps the picture was of a more youthful Britt, or the pose was more dramatic than any he could take up against a background of baize table-cloth and water-carafe. Perhaps it was simply that his most vivid recollection of the meeting was of the dark girl who had been so busy stage-managing it.

He turned the paper over. "*Youth Clubs of the N.L.P. . . . urgently in need of funds. . . donations large or small. . . . Get in touch with your local branch, or send contributions direct to Primrose Dubetat, Organising Secretary.*"

Could she be Primrose Dubetat? She looked like an organising secretary. She had certainly organised that chauffeur in the High Street a few minutes ago. A domineering woman no doubt; one of those female nuisances who always pushed and shoved themselves into the retinues of those in the public eye. Primrose Dubetat! The name suited the type, and, when you thought of it, you could only lament the disappearance of the ducking-stool as an instrument of social discipline. Of course, the Dubetat was good-looking, but that only made her more dangerous. What, by the way, would be her relationship to Arthur Lamorak-Britt? Did one need three guesses?

Peter turned back to take another look at the politician, at the expression of limpid candour and simple strength. A phoney? Possibly. And yet . . . ? Peter experienced a sudden misgiving, a vague uneasiness, as if he had wandered to a far point of rock along a cliff-walled shore, and wondered if he could get back before the tide turned. The girl came to his mind again, and he was irritated. He could not rid himself of his uneasiness.

Something pushed against his shoe, tugged at the lace. He looked down, and there was Douglas the cat come to seek attention.

He bent and stroked it.

The landlord looked across the bar. "Now then, Douglas," he said sharply. "Haven't I told you not to annoy the customers?"

Douglas leapt back on to the bar and sat down carefully among the glasses.

"Strange," said the landlord gloomily. "That cat never takes to nobody. All the world can come in. He won't let none of them touch him as a rule."

"Cats like me," Peter exclaimed, becoming a shade gloomy himself. "All cats like me."

"Strange," the landlord insisted. "Off the bar, Douglas! I had a brother named Douglas," he said. "Killed in the fourteen-eighteen. Same again, sir? Very fond of that cat I am."

Braddock returned to the bar-room and announced, as if it were not to be disputed, that it was time to go. He picked up his hat and fish, and Peter handed him the *Round Table*. Braddock stared at the eyes of Arthur Lamorak-Britt and gave a short laugh.

"Find any of the eternal truths in the rag?" he asked jovially as he led the way to the street. He was very slightly tight.

"I don't pay much attention to politics."

"Well you don't want to fall for this neo-patriotic bunkum."

The dogmatic Braddock was a new and displeasing phenomenon. Peter was tempted to bait him.

"I wouldn't call it bunkum," he said carefully. "After all, you've got to be fair. This man Britt is doing a sincere job of work. He's a good speaker. He's got magnetism. He can bring the plain Englishman to a realisation of his responsibilities."

"So you've been to one of his meetings?"

"Yes. I found it quite stimulating. It's easy to stand on one side and throw brickbats, but look at the state of the country. Something's got to be done about it."

"You think Britt can do it?" Braddock was suddenly less jovial. "Higher wages, cheaper food, reduced rents, lower income-tax, five pounds a week for everybody at sixty."

"You exaggerate."

"I don't exaggerate. I'm giving you a fair analysis. You can promise every baby the moon when you've a parliamentary representation of one."

They turned up the road and as they did so Braddock looked over his shoulder as if.... as if, Peter thought suddenly, he were being followed. "It may be a different story after the next elections," Peter argued. "I don't mean that he could get power so soon, but there's a country-wide movement behind him."

"There's a country-wide movement putting money in his purse. It's pouring in on him, from suckers like you."

"I beg your pardon!" Peter spoke sharply in protest. Braddock was looking anxiously over his shoulder again. He seemed only half aware of what he had said. Then he turned quickly. "So sorry, old man. Heat of controversy. If I was offensive, I apologise. I don't mean anything personal. I mean merely that people who don't know much about politics fall for Britt's easy line of talk. It's just as the *Sunday Gazette* says. The fellow's a charlatan, a cheap spell-binder, an opportunist."

"Perhaps you're the author of those attacks on him in the *Sunday Gazette?*"

"No, old man. I haven't gone in for newspaper work much since the war. I might do a bit more one of these days, but that's as may be. I'm sorry to upset you about Britt. I wouldn't upset you for the world." He glanced back down the lane.

Peter sighed. "You don't upset me," he lied unhappily.

"I'm glad to hear it." Braddock squared his shoulders. "I wouldn't have you fooled, either. Britt's a crook. He's in the racket for what he can get out of it. It's a fine racket, but if Mr. Britt isn't careful, it's going to break up. If the *Sunday Gazette* gets hold of the evidence it's looking for, Mr. Britt, M.P., will be out cold. All this high-falutin talk about Merry England and patriotism, all this Round Table play-acting and country conferences at Camelot – it's just a lot of hooey. Fundamentally, Britt and his gang are nothing but a bunch of crypto-fascists, and when the time comes – and it may do, what with the communists et cetera – they won't be so crypto."

"It's in the paper you bought this morning that he stands for a constitutional democracy. He wants to see England on her feet again. What's wrong with that?"

"Nothing at all. Britt's good at covering up. If he hadn't been clever, he'd have spent the last war on the Isle of Man, or maybe even in some safer place. You take my advice. Keep out of this League of Patriots, and don't hand them any of your hard-earned pelf."

Send contributions of pelf direct to Primrose Dubetat!

"I'm not joining them. I'm merely interested."

"Ah," said Braddock darkly. He glanced anxiously over his shoulder, and it was only with a visible effort that he returned to the subject. "You see, old chap, I've made a study of politics. I know the ins and outs of the game. I've picked up some snippets in my time. I could tell you things that would surprise you."

He began a long rambling story about a French politician.

Listening, Peter observed again the oddities that were becoming familiar: the pale, anxious eyes; the wisp of yellow-moustache on the pink, anxious face; the tall round-shouldered frame, the paunch, somewhat accentuated by the way in which the check tweed jacket was buttoned above it, the pigeon toes picking their way daintily over the uneven surface of the lane.

Braddock paused in his story to look behind him once more.

Irritation flashed in Peter. He interrupted: "There's no one following you," he said.

Braddock jumped and then grinned. "I was looking out for the postman, old man. Wanted to ask if he'd got a letter for me. He starts off up here you know."

True enough, the postman's round led him across the fields by a footpath off the lane before he came round to the cottage and the farm. But. . . .

"He must have passed by now."

Braddock laughed. "Think I'm fussing? Well I am. I'm expecting a nice big cheque."

"Oh, I see." Peter knew that he should feel silly and mumble an apology. He did neither. A wave of Braddock jitters had engulfed him. Braddock was lying. Very convincing that stuff about the letter with a cheque in it! But the man was lying. Peter was almost sure he was lying. There was something in the tone of voice. But why lie?

Silent, sweating slightly, Peter plodded on up the road. Either Braddock was afraid of something, or he, Peter Ackland, was heading straight for the breakdown he was here to avoid. Something must be done about it. He *must* pull himself together.

The skytip loomed ahead. A wagon was rumbling up the steep incline, its wheels clacking over the rail-joints, the steel haulage cable whipping and thumping on the track. Peter could hear faintly the whine of the motor in the distant winder-house. The wagon reached the summit. He saw the trap fall open to spill the rubble. There was a trail of grey-white dust as a sizeable fragment of rock plunged down the slope, starting a miniature avalanche.

"Damned thing!" Braddock muttered, and then, involuntarily it seemed, he looked back once more down the lane. It was a furtive, suspicious look. The look of a man expecting a cheque?

He caught Peter's eye.

"No luck," he said. But this time his grin was less convincing.

"Too bad." Peter's heart beat painfully. In a few minutes they would reach Braddock's house. There Braddock would leave him and he could put the whole silly business out of his mind. Until then he would pretend that Braddock didn't exist. Only a few more minutes.

In any case, what in the world was there for a man to be afraid of in Bosverran? Nothing . . . unless it were his own shadow.

It was not until three days later that Peter met Mr. Murrison.

Chapter 3

THERE are some men and women – not necessarily the happiest – who are able consciously to avoid the persons and the situations they find disagreeable. With Peter Ackland this was not so. He was of the guilty company of those who feel compelled to court the disagreeable out of a wretched conviction that avoidance of it is an indulgence for which a heavier price will later have to be paid.

After two days spent reclining in the Tregethneys' garden, he took himself to task. Rest had been ordered, rest without excitement; but did that mean that he was to retire altogether from the world of men? Obviously not. It was simply that he was childishly afraid that if he went abroad he might encounter Braddock. Moral cowardice? Very well, then. There was only one thing to be done. Braddock or no Braddock he would go into Bosverran the very next day and have a drink at the Green Dragon.

Once the resolution was made, the project seemed to gain in importance and attractiveness, and somehow there came to his mind the picture of a girl on the steps of the post office, a dark girl, very chic in her tweed suit. She might still be in Bosverran, or the neighbourhood. If he kept his eyes open he might see her again. It was even conceivable. . . .

No! He dismissed the thought. It was inconceivable that any girl could be a contributing factor to his restlessness. The mere suggestion was to be resented, and punctiliously he resented it, but the exercise gave him little relief.

He did not sleep well that night; and in the morning he set off up the lane with that vague feeling of depression that usually precedes a visit to the dentist. Braddock was now the sole cause of it, but Braddock's house was passed without incident, and Peter went on down the road with cheerfulness rising in him. When he reached the town, he was alert, eagerly scanning the passers-by, but there was no dark girl to turn him from his resolution, and he walked firmly through the doorway of *The Green Dragon*.

He had the bar almost to himself. He glanced at a Plymouth paper lying on the counter, stroked Douglas the cat, drank beer, and deceived himself with the reflection that here he might enjoy a moment of virtuous content. What a fool he had been the other day! How different now! Obviously the rest was beginning to do him good.

The moment came abruptly to an end. There were strangers abroad in Bosverran. Two of them. One of them, the principal, was wheezily noisy.

"Good-morning, good-morning, good-morning! How is mine host this fine morning? Have you any mead? I think I'll have a goblet of mead. It's just the weather for mead."

He laughed a hearty laugh that made him breathless. Peter Ackland recoiled. The feeling of calm was banished by a new surge of irritation. For him, the sort of humour that called a whisky and soda a goblet of mead was peculiarly offensive.

The stranger was enormously fat, a Falstaff, a colossal man, globular. His chubby pink face had rolling cheeks, and ridges of fat concealed his eyes when he laughed; china blue eyes in an innocent, baby face.

The landlord poured a glass of mead from an earthenware flask. Then Peter remembered. They really had mead in Cornwall. All right, but why call for a "goblet" of the stuff?

Peter remained hostile.

The fat man turned to his companion.

"No need to ask what you will have, Alfie. A tankard of nut-brown ale. A large tankard, landlord. A keg, if you have it."

Alfie was a small man, or so he seemed alongside the mountain. He was thin and wasp-waisted and bandy. He wore a cap. He looked like a jockey or stable-boy.

"That's right, guv," he said. "A can of beer."

The fat man lowered himself into a chair alongside the counter and glanced round.

"After all," he said jovially, "one man's mead is another man's poison." And he began consumedly to laugh.

Peter got up and left, and, as the door shut behind him, he could hear the fat man's laughter gradually turning into a sort of wheezy convulsion.

It was a disturbing sound, even alarming. It followed him long after he was out of earshot and recurred to him at odd times during the day, evoking each time the preposterous image of the fat man.

There were people like that who irritated you at first sight, who made you uneasy, and then, for no apparent cause, haunted you. Peter tried to rid himself of the incubus, but long after the encounter he still heard the wheezy laughter, and in this mental echo it had a sound of menace or warning. He told himself it was nonsense. Probably, he would never see the man again.

He was wrong.

His walk next morning took him again to Bosverran, but this time he was not lucky enough to avoid Braddock. They met in front of the fish-shop.

"Cod," said Braddock, grimly; "either that or skate. Skate! I told them what they could do with it. How have you been keeping? I always ask after you when I get the milk. Peaky, they said you'd been looking."

"I don't feel it."

"Well, that's the main thing. What about a snifter?"

They went to the Green Dragon. They had scarcely reached the bar when the fat man and the youthful Alfie came in from the street like ill-matched shadows on their heels. The fat man was heaving as if he had been hurrying, but he still had enough breath for an all-embracing greeting.

"Good-morning, good-morning!"

Braddock answered affably but casually, and turned to the landlord.

"Beer, Pascoe," he ordered. "Tall Imperial pints."

"Right, Mr. Braddock."

The fat man picked up the name. "Braddock!" he said. "Not *the* Braddock? Not Henry Braddock, the author, by any chance?"

"Yes." The author was not displeased.

"How nice! I had the hope of meeting you when I first thought of coming to Bosverran for a holiday. I'd been asking about you; intended to look you up, and here I run slap into you. Only arrived yesterday, believe it or not. It's a small world."

"I suppose it is." Even Braddock seemed overwhelmed. Peter writhed at the overflow of good humour.

The fat man clapped a heavy paw on Braddock's shoulder. "I've been wanting to talk to you ever since I read your *Study in Terrorism*. Mutual acquaintance exposed the secret of your pseudonym. Can't tell you how delighted. . . ." He wheeled ponderously. "All right, landlord, I'm paying for the drinks."

"No, no, I can't – "

"Nonsense! I'm in the chair. Have some mead. Wonderful stuff. Nothing like it."

"I'm afraid I don't care for it. If you don't mind, I'll stick to beer."

"Why should I mind?" He began to laugh. "What does the poet say? 'The bitter cup he quaffs shall eke reward him.' "

Peter shuddered. The fat man quaked, his flesh bounding. He laughed and wheezed and his pink face went scarlet. The youthful Alfie hovered anxiously. "Mind out!" he said. "Mind out now!"

"Oh dear, dear!" The fat man struggled to control himself, groped for a chair, and let himself down in it. "My sense of humour will be the death of me one of these days." He looked up as if appealing for sympathy. "Forgive me. I haven't introduced myself. My name's Murrison – Nathan M. Murrison. Queer name, isn't it? Undoubtedly a corruption of something or other. ! must go into it one of these days. I'm afraid I don't know your friend."

"Mr. Ackland," Braddock said. "From London. Taking a rest cure."

"Well, well! Londoners all, and jolly companions! Let's sit down together. This is Alfie, my valet. He looks after me wherever I go. I need a good deal of looking after. There's a lot of me."

His sense of humour was touched again. He quaked till his chair creaked; his right foot kicked under him, beating on the floor in a swift staccato ecstasy of mirth. Peter thought of the reflex action in the hind leg of a dog when you tickle the animal's spine. Mr. Murrison's laughter ended in a breathless wheezing, and another anxious admonition from the valet.

Braddock offered cigarettes. Murrison declined.

"Can't touch them, sir," he explained. "I have to stick to my own make. Herbal stuff. Stramonium." He fished with difficulty in a jacket pocket and produced a packet of cigarettes. "If I don't take care of myself, there's trouble." He tapped himself vaguely in the region of his well-covered sternum. "The heart toils less courageously than it used to do. All the time, I have, as Alfie says, to mind out. If it wasn't for Alfie, I don't know what I'd do. He's not exactly a brilliant talker, and culturally he amounts to considerably less than a row of pins, but he's a dear boy, a sweet lad."

"What's that?" Alfie inquired unexpectedly.

"I'm just explaining to the gentlemen that you have no culture, Alfie."

"Oh, that." Alfie nodded indifferently. "Anything you say."

"You see? Anything I say!"

Somewhere in it all Mr. Murrison found another irresistible flash of humour. He shook. He shook in rubbery ribs and folds, and his right foot flew at a speed an accomplished tap-dancer might have envied. It was some time before he got back to normal breathing. Then he put the asthma cigarette between his thick lips, and accepted a light from Alfie.

"You will permit me to call on you some time, Mr. Braddock," he said. "I believe I have your address. I want you to autograph a book for me. And we must have a long, long talk."

Braddock explained where he lived. Any afternoon would suit him, he said. But Mr. Murrison could not wait to bring up the subject of *A Study in Terrorism*. He suddenly became serious and sat quite still, an immovable weight, fixed forever to the enduring seat. In this mood he was not unimpressive.

Afterwards Peter was to wish that he had listened more attentively to what the fat man had said. Afterwards he was to come to the conclusion that it had all been a deliberate opening gambit, a carefully contrived piece of flattery calculated to disarm Braddock. But at the time Peter was more interested in the form, the structure, the façade of the fat man than in the talk. He heard, but did not listen. He was preoccupied with the problem of clarifying architecturally the bulk which faced him.

You could not pin down Mr. Murrison to one particular form. There were elements of the baroque in the front elevation, but the circular sweep of the whole conception was more suggestive of the Byzantine. Mr. Murrison, Peter decided, was a cross between Count Fosco and the Mosque of the Sultan Ahmed at Constantinople.

Braddock had passed from *A Study in Terrorism* to a consideration of present-day trends in Europe. Apparently Mr. Murrison took a lively interest in Balkan affairs. Possibly he had read *Yugoslavia Tomorrow*. At any rate, he was a student sitting at the feet of a master. His china blue eyes were wide open and carried an expression of earnest inquiry which was almost touching. Sometimes he looked like a puzzled child. Sometimes he was anxious, worried, as if he had a lot on his mind, like the first mate of a ship about to cast off.

They were on Tito's handling of the Croat problem when it happened.

Douglas, the cat, had approached Peter for attention and, receiving it, had rolled over on his back on the floor. Suddenly, he saw the fat man and sat up. For a moment he gazed, fascinated. Then he walked slowly towards him.

Abruptly, Murrison stopped talking.

"Alfie," he said sharply, "get that cat away! Get if away!"

He made a quick gesture of distaste, but Douglas misunderstood it. Perhaps, to an experienced cat, the enormous overspread of lap was overwhelmingly attractive. Anyway, as Alfie moved to intercept him, Douglas leaped for the lap and reached it.

What happened next was extraordinary. Murrison sprang to his feet, screaming for Alfie. The surprised cat got a grip on some trousering and clung by its claws. Murrison seized it and hurled it violently away. Douglas hit the bottom of the counter with a thud, picked himself up, and swore at the fat man with the vehemence of a veteran marine. The roused landlord came round the end of the counter in a rush, and he, too, was vehement.

"What the hell do you mean, banging my cat about?"

Murrison was gasping, tearing at his collar and tie, falling back into his chair.

"Alfie!"

It was a call for help, a cry of fear. Alfie knew what to do. He pulled a small bottle from a pocket, shook out a white tablet and slammed it into Murrison's mouth.

"There you are, guv," he said. "Take it easy. You're all right now."

"What you mean, hurting my cat?" the landlord insisted.

Alfie made a little gesture of dismissal with one hand. "Cut it out, chum," he said. "The gov'nor don't like cats. Bad for his asthma."

"I want to know what right he's got, coming in here . . ."

"I said cut it out. The cat's not hurt. You take it away from the bar before there's trouble."

"Don't you order me about! You get out of here, both of you! Nobody's going to come in here and ill-treat my cat."

Murrison was breathing more easily now as the drug took effect. His china blue eyes gazed reproachfully at the landlord. He had the hurt look of a child unjustly accused.

"I don't like this place, Alfie," he complained. "Take me out of it."

"Okay, guv." Alfie helped him to rise and held him by one elbow.

Murrison turned to Braddock. "I regret this unseemly interruption. I shall call on you, sir. I shall make it my business to find an early opportunity."

He was ponderous in his dignity, walking out, Alfie attending him, opening the swing door. The landlord's anger was cooled by amazement, and neither Braddock nor Peter was quite over his shock at the fat man's sudden violence. Only Douglas, cleaning himself up after his crash landing, seemed indifferent to that fantastic exit.

"What's the matter with the fellow?" the landlord demanded. "Is he mad?"

Peter shrugged. "Allergic to cats. Asthmatics sometimes are."

"You mean to say, just because Douglas went near him, he had that choking fit?"

"Psychological," Braddock asserted solemnly. "Some cat affected him, so he gets a horror of cats. He could work himself up so that the sight of a cat might bring on a fit."

"Well, I don't want him working himself up in my house," declared the landlord. "He's a bad man, that fellow. He meant to kill that cat. I saw it in his eyes."

"He lost his temper." Peter shrugged again. "Or got in a panic. It's not nice to suffer from asthma."

The landlord shook his head. "There was more than that to it. I saw it in his eyes. He's a bad man."

Braddock snorted. "Don't talk nonsense, Pascoe. You're so damned fond of that cat, you don't know what you're saying. You'll be getting an allergy yourself soon – an allergy to customers. Come on, Ackland. One for the road."

Peter declined. He had had enough. A revulsion was suddenly on him, a revulsion against the place and everything in it, including the innocent cat. He wanted to get away, out into the air. He wanted to get away from Braddock, but inevitably the fellow must cling to him, and inevitably they trudged up the road together to the house by the skytip. Then, as he went on alone down the lane to the farm, he had a feeling of great relief.

It lasted until after he had had his lunch. He sat down to read, but he was restless, and soon got up again. He had an unaccountable fear that Braddock might come looking for him. The thought was oppressive. The possibility must be avoided.

He took his hat and stick and walked out into the heart of the clay country, to a hill from which he could look out over the scarred and pimpled landscape. The gleaming cones of the skytips drew a wide ring round him, and far in the distance he could see the similar cones of the St. Austell workings. He felt safe here from Braddock. He hoped he might meet Tom Hicks, whom he knew through the Tregethneys.

Tom was the head or "captain" of the widest and deepest pit thereabouts, and there wasn't much Cap'n Hicks didn't know about clay. He was a talkative old boy when he had a good audience; and Peter, who always fed him with questions at the end of the lecture, was very good. He had found the subject of china clay and the soft Cornish voice of Cap'n Hicks very soothing. So that now, standing on the edge of the great pit of Bosverran Number Three, he knew the meaning of everything he saw.

Cap'n Hicks had explained it all, and Peter had gone with him along the narrow cat-walks between the settling tanks, following the clay to the long, steamy sheds of the dries. But the fascination was in the pit, not in the process; in the shuttling up and down of the wagons, or "skips", as the men called them. He would stand on the edge of the spectacular hole and watch the wagons being loaded by those miniature figures on the floor. Each wagon looked like a toy truck. But each had a capacity of a ton and a quarter, and each, when loaded, would begin its swift journey along the tram-track, hauled by steel rope up the long incline to the surface, and so on up to the top of the great skytip.

One day Peter had climbed to the top, where the lip-man had his lonely post, and up there you got a different view of the wagon. It would come rattling and rumbling along its rails, the noise rising in swift crescendo in the final spurt to the pinnacle. Then a mechanical device would cause a trap to open, the load of rock and smaller rubble would shoot out, and the trap would snap shut with a clanging action that made Peter think of a guillotine.

He had gone, also, to the winder-house a quarter of a mile away, from which the cable system of the wagons was operated by the motorman. Bell signals would clang, motors would whine and indicators would begin to travel round dials to show the positions of the rising and descending wagons. He got more facts from the motorman: the size of the drum on which the steel rope was wound, how the clutch worked, the nature of the brake, the efficiency of the starter apparatus. The motorman was eager to explain.

Most of the skytips, both near and far, looked as if they had been turned out of one master mould, though, if you measured them, you would find they differed in size. In their growth and shape they conformed to a natural law, and, if you asked Cap'n Hicks about it, he would talk of the angle of repose. The angle of repose was forty-three degrees – or was it forty-five? The rails on which the wagons ran always projected a little over the tip, reaching out into space, and it was from the projecting part that the rubble fell, so there was nothing to hinder it from finding its natural angle of repose.

Weathering affected the shape of some of the older tips; irregularities might also be caused by the removal of some of the waste. Otherwise, it was only when some emergency required a shift in the dumping apparatus that the mound departed from the normal. A sand-slide might endanger the pit; on the other hand, the skytip might threaten a road or private property. Or the direction of the dumping incline might be changed so that a productive clay lode could be followed.

All this information and more Peter absorbed with the peculiar avidity that really useless knowledge sometimes stimulates. He could not know how much it was going to matter to him. All it meant to him at the time was that the details of the scene he surveyed had significance for him. He was no longer a stranger in the land. He could read the signs. For instance, that wide step-like ledge that marred the regularity of the skytip in the middle distance was the result of a shift in the dumping rails. Without that shift, the tip would have buried the road that traversed, with so many bends and doublings back, the whole area of the clay-pits. It was somehow entertaining to know this.

There was a car running along the road towards the irregular skytip as Peter looked out from his eminence that day. He thought at first it might be Cap'n Hicks' car, but when it came nearer he saw that it was not. He watched it idly then, until it disappeared behind the mound. He rather wanted to find Hicks; not for anything special, just for a talk.

He walked round the rim of the pit to the winder-house and looked in at the doorway. The place was nothing more than a stone-built shed, and the big cable-drum and the motor filled most of the space. The engine hummed and the drum rumbled as it turned, and outside a loaded skip came rattling up the incline, passing an empty one that was on its way to the pit floor. The man in charge of the shed sat in front of his signal discs and gripped the handle that controlled the speed of the skips. Peter had to wait till the brake was applied before he could ask a question.

"Cap'n 'Icks? 'Ee be gone over to Maalvean pit, I do believe."

The bell rang. The man manipulated his clutch and swung the control handle.

Peter picked his way across the rough land to the pit called Maalvean, but there was no sign of Cap'n Hicks. He gave up. It was getting late, and a turn in the weather was threatening; time he returned to the farm. He had had enough of cross-country trudging, so he decided to follow the road from Maalvean.

To call it a road was to flatter it. It was a rubble track, powdery with grey-white clay dust. It took him past the irregular skytip he had seen from the hill. He had not been that way before, so he paused to have a look at the pit.

It was not being worked, though obviously kept in trim for a resumption of work at any time. Looking down at the floor, he could see wagons that the last shift had loaded; wagons waiting to be carried skyward. Perhaps the pit was uneconomical. These loaded skips in the deep gulch suggested a sudden order to stop work. There had been one sand-slide, but that must have been years ago. The dump had been piled up high since the shift of the track. The ridge that flanked the great cone was the weathered remnant of the original tip. It was like a giant step, a lower plateau, halfway up the side of the cone. That was curious. Peter made a mental note to ask Cap'n Hicks about it.

Rounding the cone, he came upon the car he had seen from the hill. It was empty, drawn up in the rough at the side of the road. He looked round, but the whole land seemed as empty of life as the car. He looked up. The great cone of rubble and rock towered above him. At this angle it seemed colossal, even menacing. A new feeling.

Peter shook himself. It wouldn't do. He was going the way of Braddock, letting these mounds get on his nerves. It was all nonsense, of course. It could be nothing more than the emptiness of the land, the loneliness of gouged and tortured earth. The car, far from being an earnest of life, seemed to accentuate the deathliness of the solitude.

No good shaking himself. No good standing there stupidly. Do something. Lay the ghost!

The car was an Austin Twelve, near the retiring age. He walked over and put his hand on the warm radiator.

Perhaps Hicks had borrowed this car, his own having broken down.

Peter looked through the window. There was nothing of the pit captain's usual gear on the back seat. There was nothing in the car.

The upholstery was scratched and worn. In one place a spring protruded.

Peter went back towards the pit, still thinking of Hicks. The winder-house was set only a few yards from the rim and right under the shadow of the skytip. You had to cross a crazy trestle bridge to get to it, a bridge thrown over the tram-track that ran from the floor of the pit to the top of the dump.

As he rounded the base of the dump, he looked towards the winder-house. He saw a movement in the doorway. The figure of a man appeared for a moment, then drew back.

If the movement seemed covert, surreptitious, it must surely be an illusion. No one was likely to go to that engine-shed without a good reason. No doubt there was an inspection in progress. The man in the doorway had been called back. It might have been Hicks himself. At the distance, identification was difficult. Now Peter was much nearer, but the man did not reappear.

Peter hesitated at the bridge. A broken, rusted wagon had been hauled from the incline and left at the side of the road, a castaway.

He listened. There was no sound in the land. Not a rustle of gorse, not a bird cry. The hum of motors and the rattle of wheels on the tracks of even the working pits had ceased. It was crib-time, the mid-shift break.

The shadow of the cone and its ledge was reaching across the wilderness, falling across the wall of the pit.

Peter crossed the sagging plank-and-handrail bridge and walked up to the open door of the winder-house. Then he remembered that he was trespassing. Some officer of the company inside the shed might challenge his right to wander on the property,

"Is Captain Hicks there?" he asked loudly, claiming some authority from his familiarity with Hicks.

"Captain Hicks?" a drawling voice echoed. "Wouldn't know him from General Gordon. Why, if it isn't Mister – wait a minute, I'll get it! Ackland, Mr. Ackland!"

Peter stared. Confronting him, a surprising and weighty apparition, was Mr. Nathan M. Murrison, and beyond, on the driver's platform, hovered Alfie, the valet.

Mr. Murrison laughed. He laughed and quaked flabbily, and his right foot was restless as if it wanted to start tap-dancing.

"Oh, dear, dear!" he panted. "You nearly frightened Alfie to death, Mr. Ackland. He thought you were going to charge us with trespass. Mistook you for a foreman or something. We've no right in this shed, of course, but I'm always so curious to know how things work. Aren't you? Do you think these clay people really would mind our taking a peep? Alfie thinks we should have asked permission, but he's such a timid soul. He gets in a panic if anyone says boo to him. You get in a panic, don't you, Alfie?"

The little, jockey-like man came from behind the starting-gear of the motor and down the steps from the platform. He seemed very bandy on the steps. His small eyes were screwed up as if he were riding into a wind, but Peter saw a venomous flicker in them as they looked him over. Alfie was quite a few furlongs from panic.

"All right, guv," he said. "Let's get on."

Murrison ignored the suggestion. "I never imagined these clay-pits could be so exciting, Mr. Ackland. We came out here by sheer chance, as it were. Rambling, you might say. Alfie wanted to see what was doing, but we seem to have struck a disused pit. It is disused, isn't it?"

"I can't say I know much about it. I was wondering myself."

"Come on, guv," Alfie said. "Let's go."

"Don't be so tiresome, Alfie!" The fat man was more hurt than annoyed. "I don't pay you to be tiresome."

"It's getting late."

"Never mind if it is getting late. What I want to know is: do I pay you to be tiresome?"

For a moment the small man was quite still; but when he did speak, his tone was mild.

"I better start the car," he said, and, passing Peter in the doorway, made for the bridge with quick, bandy strides.

"Temperamental!" Mr. Murrison shook his head regretfully, and he wore his hurt child look. "Sometimes I'm at my wits' end, Mr. Ackland. I take from him what I would take from no other servant – from no other man! I put up with his uncouth ways. I treat him almost as an equal, but he has no appreciation, Mr. Ackland. He fails to realise that I am more like a friend than an employer. And some day it will be too late. Some day I shall be at the end of my patience, and then, heaven knows what will become of him. Or of me, for that matter. He looks after me as if I were all he had in the world, so I try to curb my natural impatience."

Peter was embarrassed by the confidence. A little puzzled, too, for the china blue eyes of the fat man seemed to be peering inside him, trying to estimate how he was taking it.

"I trust you appreciate the situation, Mr. Ackland?"

What could it possibly matter to the fellow whether he appreciated it or not? For a moment he countered the blue gaze with a probing stare of his own. He had a twinge of uneasiness, as if there were something wrong with the whole scene. Phoney was the word in his mind. Mr. Murrison was at such great pains to explain the behaviour of his valet. It was almost as if he feared that the nature of the relationship might be questioned. Perhaps it should be!

The horn of the car blared angrily, peremptorily.

"You see what I mean?" The fat man frowned, then decided to take it as a joke. The mounds and folds of his face were called on to accommodate the coils of a small smile, a tentative, anxious smile.

"We're returning to Bosverran," he said. "Can we give you a lift?"

"Thanks. If you're taking the top road, you could drop me at Trevone Farm."

When they came to the car, the engine was running and Alfie sat at the wheel. He didn't move. He had his mouth clamped shut as if nothing would get it open.

"Tell him how to get to your farm, Mr. Ackland," Murrison requested.

Alfie said nothing in acknowledgment of the directions. He let in the clutch before Murrison could close the door. In the back seat the fat man nudged Peter and began to laugh. He went through the usual quakings and foot-tapings, but the laugh seemed as false as his recent apology for Alfie. Peter's uneasiness now was more than a twinge. There was something peculiar about this Murrison-Alfie set-up; something about the pair that made him regret his decision to ride with them. There was something not quite healthy here: something very far from the kind of joke over which Mr. Murrison laughed so consumedly. An odour of cruelty, perhaps? That was it! Cruelty.

Suddenly Peter Ackland was afraid, and as suddenly the emotional bankrupt emerged. He had given himself into the hands of these two and he would be no match for them if they attacked him. They could stun him and rob him and toss him into the clay dust of the road. Or they could carry him away, out of the district and turn him loose after taking his money. He had walked into a trap, an elaborate trap. They had seen him wandering among the clay-pits, had waited for him in the winder-house with their script prepared. Desperately, he invoked reason to clear his mind, but reason was helpless. The fear was all-pervading, and would not succumb to logic. It was true that the driver had taken the top road, just as directed, but there was little reassurance in this. The top road was a lonely track across the upper wilderness of bracken and gorse and tumbled granite, a winding way among the pits and skytips, where violence could be done with no witness under the clouds.

Only recently a man had disappeared. The newspapers had been full of it. He had walked out of his place of business and disappeared. The police had circulated a photograph and a description. A pedestrian had come forward to say that he had seen the scared face of a man looking out from the window of a speeding car. There had been two other men in the car with him. It might have been an Austin Twelve. This car, these two. . . .

There was no one along the clay-dusted roads to see a scared face looking out.

The fat man groped with a fat hand towards his jacket pocket. He grunted, swivelling a little on the broken springs, to get his hand into the pocket. The car bounced and lurched, and bounced again.

Peter braced himself, waiting for the fat hand to emerge. He had a sensation of a prickling band drawn across his brow. He had never faced a man with a gun. He was afraid, but resolved to fight, ready to make a wild grab and wrench the gun away. It was coming. The elbow lifted. Now.

With a jerk and a grunt Mr. Murrison pulled a silk handkerchief from his pocket and wiped his thick lips. He nudged Peter again, pointed at the driver's back, drew his mouth down in a mimicry of sulks, then went off into one of his laughing fits.

Peter, with great effort, turned on a smile. He was a knot of embarrassment, a shrinking, hardening knot.

Alfie drove on grimly, pressing the engine hard. The car was running down hill now, and round the next bend was Trevone Farm. Peter made another effort.

"Pull up at the white gate please," he instructed Alfie, hoping that his voice had the casual sound he intended.

Murrison was still heaving, but got control of himself as Alfie braked to a halt. It wasn't easy for him to move his bulk from the car, yet he insisted on struggling out ahead of Peter.

"Is that Braddock's house on the next rise?" he asked.

"That's it."

"Good fellow, Braddock," the fat man remarked. "Close friend of yours?"

Peter shook his head. "I scarcely know him. Just a chance meeting."

"Brilliant man!" The china blue eyes had a baby-like earnestness. "I've followed his career. Never has found the public he deserves. Perhaps . . ." A movement of his shoulders suggested a shrug. "I shall be seeing you again, I hope. Take care of yourself. Beware the night air."

"Thanks for the lift."

Peter watched the car go up the lane, saw it stop at Braddock's cottage. He still felt a hot-faced embarrassment, and stood there, blaming himself for a fool. First Braddock; now Murrison. Did he have to imagine a gun every time a man put a hand in a pocket? If this sort of thing went on, soon he'd be ducking whenever a woman opened a handbag. The doctor had been right, by Jove! He was worse than he had thought. He must relax more, rest, empty his mind, stop imagining strange things about people.

Relax now, walk into the house quite casually. Take it easy. There! Sam Tregethney hasn't set up a Lewis gun in the parlour. Mrs. Tregethney has put away the cyanide for to-day.

He looked out of the window, up the lane again. The car was still in front of Braddock's cottage. Mr. Murrison was making a call. The great cone of waste from the neighbouring clay-pit looked very white against a smoky sky. The afternoon had been fine, but there was no good promise for the night. A storm was coming up out of the Atlantic to end the day's tranquillity.

Chapter 4

It must have been soon after eight when the note arrived.

Darkness had brought the storm with it. The farmhouse was snug enough but, to Peter, surprisingly noisy. The wind thudded against the thick walls and moaned or belched moodily in the chimneys. On the west side of the house it whistled and sighed through every crack. When the rain squalls came the gusts hurled the drops against the windows like gravel. The whole place creaked like a ship at sea.

He found all these sounds curiously troubling. After dinner, he sat in the small sitting-room trying to read; but his attention kept wandering from his book to the gale outside. Tregethney had referred to it indifferently as a "bit of a blow" and of no consequence to his broccoli, but in Peter's mind it was beginning to assume the proportions of a West-Indian hurricane. Then he heard footsteps outside.

For a moment he thought that they must belong to Tregethney going round the house to one of the outbuildings; but a moment or two later there was a ring at the kitchen door and a murmur of voices. Then the footsteps began again, returning the way they had come, and the sitting-room door opened. Mrs. Tregethney came in.

"There's a letter for you, Mr. Ackland. Mr. Ferry's cowman brought it." She gave him a blue envelope. "He wouldn't wait for an answer," she added from the door, "nor for you to give him a little something for himself. He's a grumpy sort of man with no manners to speak of."

"Thank you, Mrs. Tregethney." Peter looked at the letter. Ferry's was the next farm to the Tregethneys' and nearer to Bosverran. His first thought had been that the postman had delivered it there by mistake. But it was unstamped and over his name, written and underlined with an elaborate flourish, was the word URGENT. He opened it.

"My Dear Peter Ackland, [he read]
"I hope to be off to London first thing in the morning, and I would like to see you. I wouldn't drag you out, only it's very important and I'm up to my eyes in packing and what-not. By the way, I've got that book I promised you. I'll be waiting.

"Sincerely,
"Henry Braddock."

Peter's first impulse was to tear up the note and forget about it. Good heavens, didn't the man realise what a night this was? He'd be waiting, would he? That was very good of him! Well, he could wait all night if he wanted to. Sincerely, Peter Ackland.

It took him some minutes to change his mind; minutes of failing to disregard the storm, of arguing that a walk in the wind might do him good, of arriving at the conclusion that Braddock might really have something important to say or ask. But the thought was depressing, and he still hesitated. At last he put his book down, donned a raincoat, crammed his hat lightly on his head and battled his way up the lane. By the time he reached Braddock's house his depression had gone like one of the clouds he could see tearing away from the face of the moon. He was almost glad he had come. He had quite forgotten Braddock.

There were lights downstairs in the house. He was nearly lifted off his feet by the gale as he turned the corner of the building, but it propelled him into the shelter of the lee side. He paused to get his breath, then, taking hold of the badly hung knocker, he banged on the door.

The porch was a pocket of silence. The night streamed by noisily. He waited, listening to the rush of the storm. He knocked again, then heard Braddock shouting against the noise, shouting from the darkness of an upstairs room.

"Who's that?"

The high-pitched voice had a nervous tightness.

Peter shouted his reply.

"You, Ackland!" The relief in the man's tone was dearly audible. "Wait a jiff! I'll let you in."

What followed reminded Peter of his first call at the cottage. There was the same drawing back of bolts, the same rattle of the guard-chain, the same look of nervous tension only just relaxed.

"Come in, old man. Delighted to see you. Afraid you wouldn't turn up. Hang your coat on a peg. Do you know what the time is? My clock has stopped."

Peter took off his coat and glanced at his watch.

"Eight thirty-three."

"I thought it was later." Braddock bolted and chained the door. "The storm brought on the night so early."

"Why so much locking?" Peter asked.

"Yes, I suppose it is stupid. Sort of habit. Living in foreign parts so much. Come into the kitchen. Do you mind? It's cosier."

The kitchen was a mess. The cleaning woman hadn't been in for two days, and dishes were piled high on the draining board. The table was a clutter of used plates and cutlery, shoe-brushes, saucepans, all sorts of odds and ends. A percolator burped on the slab of the Cornish range and the aroma of coffee filled the overheated room. There was another odour, less agreeable. Peter sniffed twice before he identified it: the smell of burned resin flux. Then he saw among the paraphernalia on the table a Primus stove and a soldering-iron. There were flattened splashes of solder shining on the table.

Braddock picked up the iron and looked for another place to put it. "Been mending a saucepan," he announced.

"Going to take it to London with you?"

Braddock looked startled, then laughed. But he did not answer the question. It seemed there was no other place for the soldering iron. He put it back on the table.

"Beer or coffee?" he said.

"Coffee, thanks."

"Oh, here . . ." Braddock abstracted a book from beneath some debris on the dresser ". . . that's the book I promised you."

"Thank you very much. Very kind of you."

It was *A Study in Terrorism* and was in the state described in booksellers first edition catalogues as "stains on covers, handled, but a good copy." One of the stains was egg.

Braddock found two clean cups. "As a matter of fact, it's pretty rare now. Out of print. Time there was a cheap edition." He was looking for the sugar. He found it and hooked out a splash of solder with a dirty spoon. "I told the publishers quite firmly. 'Keep it in print,' I said, 'or you lose the rights.' That's in my contract of course. They're very valuable, these rights," he added. "Milk?"

"No thanks."

"As a matter of fact," said Braddock, "the author's position is a very difficult one just now."

He went on to talk about the author's position. Peter sipped his coffee. It wasn't bad coffee, not bad at all. As a matter of fact – to use Braddock's favourite, somewhat shifty phrase – it made a pleasant interlude between two encounters with a Cornish gale. Somewhere or other they built hurricane-proof houses, didn't they? Interesting! For a while he was only half aware of what Braddock was saying. Some phrases penetrated: "paper situation," "ascending royalty scales," "tax position," "six-monthly statements," "unimaginative policy". Suddenly, he became attentive – attentive and wary. The direction of Braddock's monologue had changed.

"So you see how it is," he was saying. "I've simply got to run up to London for a few days and sort things out. It places me in a very difficult position. As I said, things haven't been going too well. There isn't the money about. So I've got to do something about getting what they owe me. I don't like it, naturally, but the money's there and it looks as if I shall have to go after it. Newspapers! I never did like dealing with them. Tricky lot."

"I suppose so."

"But it's a devil of a spot to be in. Those that want can't have. You know how it is. Mark you, I had thought of sending them a wire demanding my fare, but one has one's pride. Besides, it wouldn't get to the right man. Some little pip-squeak of an assistant editor would get it, and not knowing the facts – which would embarrass him if he did know – turn it down."

Peter had it now. It was a touch. For an instant he wanted to laugh. Disdaining the conventional approach or, perhaps, not wishing to get his feet wet, Braddock the Bold, the student of politics, had summoned his prospective lamb to the slaughter with a note.

"So you see," Braddock was saying, "I've simply got to see this man. Then I'll be all right. There's a lot of money coming to me, but if I don't go after it, the thing may drag on for months."

"Yes?" Peter wasn't going to help him.

"I suppose," said Braddock as if the idea had only just occurred to him; "I suppose you couldn't manage a few pounds, could you?"

"Well . . ."

"Look, old chap, I wouldn't dream of asking you if I weren't desperate. And it's only for a few days."

"Can't you write to this man?"

"No use. I've tried. I've got to see him personally. Once he knows the hole I'm in, he'll write me a cheque. There's no doubt of it, old chap. It's as safe as the Bank of England."

He stood there on the other side of the table, teetering on his pigeon toes. He was desperate. He was frightened. That was the queer thing in him, the obvious fear of something, and something more ominous than a line-up of duns. There was a curious note in his voice, and his pale eyes had a kind of cornered-animal appeal in them. They were not the things this man could act.

"Besides, it's urgent. I must be on the train tomorrow morning. It's only for a few days, old man. Ill pay you back the minute I return."

"I'd like to help, but I'm very short." Peter lowered his gaze and scowled at the table. Why did he have to feel guilty? Even if not strictly truthful, the excuse was not unreasonable. Yet his own ears heard in it a whine worse than that in Braddock's plea. He could not even look

Braddock in the eyes. He saw the mess of things on the table, the used plates, the sooted pots, the frying-pan with the remains of a nice bit of fish, the bright splashes of solder, and a copy of the *Round Table* with the face of Arthur Lamorak-Britt gazing up from it at the smoky ceiling.

A sighing breath of despair came from Braddock.

"Look, old chap, a tenner will see me through nicely. A few days, and I'll be rolling in it. I don't want to press you, but Tregethney could cash a cheque for you. If you could manage a tenner, I'd gladly pay you for the accommodation. An extra fiver. More, if you like."

"Don't be absurd!"

"All right, forget it." Braddock lowered himself to a chair, scared, forlorn, beaten. "I wouldn't have asked you, only there's no one else I could go to."

Peter produced his wallet and counted out ten notes. Braddock wasn't looking. Walls had closed in on him. He was an abject prisoner, pitiful in his isolation. Peter got up to go. He folded the notes and pushed them across the table.

"Ten pounds you said."

He had a feeling of relief, but it was by no means unalloyed. He turned away. He did not want to see the man's face. He caught Braddock's reaction only in his words.

"My God! I thought you were turning me down."

"Never mind what you thought."

"You don't know what this means to me. You've saved my life. I'll be able to go up by the morning train. I'll pack a few . . ." He broke off abruptly and sprang to his feet. He was alert, almost spry. He had shed the look of anxious fear. The ten pounds had opened a door to him.

"Good Lord, yes!" he exclaimed, as if a new thought had come as a triumphant achievement. "I could even go to-night. Look, old chap, I could pick up the night train at Par. There's plenty of time. Plenty. Once I'm on that train I'll be safe."

"Safe?"

The questioning echo of his word pulled Braddock up. He seemed startled, embarrassed, caught out.

"I mean everything will be all right. Do me one more favour, old chap. Telephone Ben Stevens while I chuck a few things in a suitcase. I hate to bother you, but I must catch that train. You could call him from the Commercial Hotel. That's the nearest 'phone. You'll find his number in the book. Tell him I want to catch the ten-twenty-five from Par, and have him knock three times when he gets here. It's an awful night, I know, but you're well wrapped-up and it's not far to the Commercial. Drop in on your way back, so I'll know it's all right. Just knock three times yourself, and I'll let you in."

Peter didn't even think of protesting. Since he had advanced the money for the trip, the whole thing suddenly seemed to be his responsibility. Underlying his acquiescence may have been the desire to get rid of Braddock, to ship him off to London and gain a respite; but if so he was unaware of it. He merely felt in some way committed.

He walked into the night of wind and rain and struggled past the great white mound along the road to Bosverran. He knew the lay-out at the Commercial. He had gone in there once or twice. The telephone was in a little passage between the bar and the darts room, and you asked for the book at the counter. Someone was using the instrument when he entered, and he heard one side of a domestic conversation that was becoming monosyllabic and somewhat heated. There were a few solemn drinkers at tables in the bar. The livelier patrons were following the usual pattern of Bosverran night-life in the darts room, from which came spasmodic noises of approval or derision.

Peter bought a half-pint of bitter and looked up the number. When he got to the telephone, he had to wait fully a minute before Ben Stevens answered. The connection was bad, but, with a little shouting and some repetition, he delivered his message. Ben Stevens said it would be okay. He'd pick up Mr. Braddock in time to catch the London train at Par.

Another customer was waiting in the passage to use the telephone. Peter had some vague idea that the man had come from the darts room. He muttered a mechanical "sorry" as he relinquished the instrument, but he didn't feel sorry, he felt irritated because the fellow had hung around in the passage, right at his elbow. There might be nothing private about his call for a car, but this emphasis on the lack of privacy annoyed him none the less, and he was scowling when he returned to the bar to pay for his call and finish his beer.

Two new arrivals were drinking at the counter: Mr. Murrison and Alfie. The fat man beamed; his boyish henchman was not so pleased.

"I thought I recognised your voice," Mr. Murrison wheezed. "Do I understand you were 'phoning for a taxi to take you to Par?"

"No, you're mistaken." All Peter's annoyance went into the retort, and he turned abruptly to pay twopence to the barman.

Mr. Murrison was hurt. From the mournful look in his china blue eyes he might have been deeply hurt.

"I merely wished to offer my own poor car in case of need," he answered; "to obtrude myself was farthest from my thoughts."

Peter apologised, but not very warmly. He found the prospect of Mr. Murrison's remaining hurt surprisingly easy to contemplate.

"You're very kind," Peter said; "but I wasn't getting a car for myself."

Murrison responded like an obscene flower to the light. He beamed round again. "I'm glad to hear that. I'm looking forward to our better acquaintance. Don't tell me Mr. Braddock's leaving us unexpectedly?"

"He'll be back," Peter said. "He's just going to London for a few days."

"Oh, dear, dear! How unfortunate. My own holiday down here is necessarily short, but it can't be helped. What are you drinking, Mr. Ackland?"

"Nothing more, thanks. I must be on my way."

"Come, come! A minute or two won't alter the course of your life. There's plenty of time for Par, if you're running over with Braddock?"

"No, I think he's quite capable of getting on a train by himself. But . . ."

"Well, then, there's no need to rush. Let me buy you a glass of mead. It's very good here. A nice place altogether. Very comfortable, and no cats."

Mr. Murrison began to laugh, but stopped abruptly, with mouth open. He struggled for breath, his face reddening quickly.

"Mind out, guv!" Alfie snapped. "Mind out!"

Murrison gripped the edge of the counter, bending over. Alfie was feeling in a pocket for the ephedrine bottle, but this time it was not needed. The fat man got his breath back.

"This cursed affliction," he complained. "Never know when it's going to get you. Avoid asthma, Mr. Ackland. It's the plague of plagues."

Mr. Ackland buttoned up the collar of his mackintosh. "I must get home while the rain holds off," he said firmly.

"Look in tomorrow. Alfie and I will be here."

"Splendid," said Peter vaguely. "Good night." He went. It was good to get out into the wind.

The moon had gone again. The rain waited till he was just clear of the town and on the long stretch of open road. Then it came pelting down, and there was no shelter anywhere. His coat protected as much of him as it covered, but that wasn't enough. His hat was quickly a sodden, useless mess. From his knees down he was so wet that he might have been wading. The wind was behind him, but it was still a wind, and the flying rain-drops lashed his neck. He felt the centre of a liquid world. Then, the wind drove the storm eastward and the torrent passed. Overhead the clouds broke, and when the moon came out in a sky of tattered streamers, the night had grandeur. It had weirdness, too, a Brocken weirdness. For some people there were witches cloud-hopping up there; but not for Peter. He missed the grandeur and the weirdness. He was conscious only of acute discomfort, of sodden trousers and squelching shoes. He was tired and wretched.

Three knocks on the door. That, perhaps, was an old Yugoslav custom. One for a Titoist, two if you favoured Moscow, three for a snooping scribbler.

Peter banged on the door as if he meant to make an end of the thing.

The bolts rattled, the chain clinked. Peter looked round to see if there were any spies glowering green-eyed from behind the veronicas.

It was just the night for them.

"All right," he snapped at Braddock. "Stevens is going to pick you up."

"Come in, old chap. Come in. I've made some fresh coffee."

"I'm wet through. I'm going home to get a hot bath."

"Won't you stay till Stevens comes. I wish you would. It won't put you out much more."

There was no end to it. Lend him money, run his errands, sit with him and hold his hand! He exploded.

"Damn it all, look at the state I'm in! What the hell are you afraid of?"

"Don't be silly, old chap! What should I be afraid of?" Braddock rocked in the doorway on his pigeon-toed feet. "I just wanted to talk to you for a moment."

"I'm going home to get a bath. I've had enough for one night."

"All right, old chap, if you put it that way." Braddock stared anxiously past him into the tattered night. "There's just one small favour I'd like to ask. Send on my mail for me, will you? Just the letters. Don't bother about papers or parcels. Here's a spare key for you. All you'll have to do is open this door and pick the stuff up from the mat. Parcels are left in the porch. If there should be any, bung them in the hall here. I'll be at Pero's Hotel, Gladdon Street. I've written it down for you."

Peter kept his hands in his coat pockets, ignoring the key and the card.

"You've got a woman who comes in to clean. Surely she can look after your mail."

"I can't have her in the house while I'm away. She's not trustworthy." The pitch of Braddock's voice rose with his anxiety. "You pass every day, old man. I wouldn't ask if it was going to be any trouble for you. It's just the letters. There may be something important."

Peter sighed and shrugged. "All right," he said. "Give me the key." He took the key and the card with the address. "I'll be back in a few days," Braddock assured him. "There'll be nothing to bother you."

"I hope your business goes well. Good-bye."

"Good-bye. I can't begin to thank you."

"That's all right."

They shook hands.

When Peter looked back from the gate, Braddock was standing in the lighted hall, a paunchy, ungainly figure, with that unstable pigeon-toed stance. He held his hands close together in front of him, thrust forward, as if he were pushing his way through some dense jungle. He groped for the doorknob as if to steady himself. Then he closed the door.

That was the last time Peter saw him alive.

Chapter 5

HE slept badly that night. The storm made him restless. The wind howled and whooped and the rain rattled like pellets on the skin of a side-drum. In London you weren't conscious of such weather. There might be several floors between you and the roof, and, though the wind would buffet your window-panes, its force never seemed as great as this. Here, in this wild country, in this small farmhouse, the storm seemed right on top of you. There was nothing to impede it. All the weather of the wide Atlantic was scooped up and hurled across Cornwall. It might whip the roof away at any moment. It might topple the chimneys and breach the walls. It seemed impossible that the thin glass of the windows could hold.

For long periods Peter was conscious of listening to the noise, all the noises. They would die away for a moment, then rise swiftly to a screaming fortissimo, a chorus of disorder. He listened till he had a feeling of disintegration in himself. When he was desperate, unable to resist it any more, there came a respite, a pool of quiet. He actually heard the drip of water from the eaves. Then he heard nothing. He dozed.

He did not know when the storm began again. The noise of it woke him. Then, again there was a lull. And so it went on through the night, till the gale blew itself out and there was only an occasional gust straggling in its wake. The intervals of silence grew longer.

Silence. From far off he heard the whine and rattle of a wagon ascending the incline of a skytip.

The thing seemed so real, he jerked up in bed to listen. It was impossible, of course. Through the window he saw the faint grey smudge of a watery dawn. The pit men wouldn't be at work for hours yet. The noise he had heard must have been an echo in his mind. Or he had been dreaming.

"They get on your nerves, those damned skytips. Live among them long enough, and you begin to dream about them."

He hadn't paid much attention to Braddock's complaint, but perhaps there was something in it after all.

He closed his eyes, and then it seemed to him that he sprang suddenly from the darkness of sleep into a box of sunlight.

The clock on the side table said it was eight. He listened a while before he got up. No sound but the birds. It was still too early for the wagons. He tried to shake off the dream – for dream it must have been – but it wasn't easy. It had seemed real. And for no rational reason it troubled him.

He missed Braddock. He had not liked the man, but now that he would not see him for a few days, he regretted his surliness at the time of their parting. Not that it mattered much, because after all Braddock hadn't gone to the ends of the earth. Not even to Yugoslavia; merely on a brief visit to London. Curious fellow, Braddock. However infuriating he might be, there was a kind of haplessness about him that carried an appeal. In his absence you could think of him not so much as a questionable professional adventurer, but rather as a boy in search of experience. He might be older than you, but from your adult superiority, your accumulated wisdom of thirty-five years, you saw in him the pathos of youth, the sad earnestness of one who still stumbled through the testing years, who would go on stumbling. There it was, you couldn't help it, you pitied him.

The sun shone gaily after the storm. The clean Atlantic air was delicious, and Peter Ackland might have slept soundly all through the night for all the weariness he felt once he had got outside and stretched his limbs on the walk up the lane to Braddock's house.

There was no mail to send on this first day. He was mildly disappointed, and realised that he had been looking forward to the small service as a reparation for his ungracious behaviour.

The hall was in a mess. Papers, apparently from a carved oak chest that stood with its lid open, had been tossed over the floor; papers and books, some old clothes. A loud check sports jacket with a great rent in the lining lay over one end of the chest. Apparently Braddock had made a frantic last minute search for something in the chest, and, in his haste, had pitched things anywhere. The man really was impossible. Peter shut the door and turned the key.

He walked down the road into Bosverran. He had become familiar with the faces of many people in the town, but this morning they were all strangers to him. He felt curiously lost. There were never many cars in Bosverran. However, he looked up and down the High Street, suddenly interested in cars. Then he realised that what he was really looking for was a big cream-coloured saloon with the emblem of *Excalibur* on the door. He went off busily to the post office to buy some stamps. He stayed a while. He read a notice about health insurance. He examined the electoral register for the division. His name wasn't on it, naturally. Neither was the name of Miss Primrose Dubetat. And no dark girl in tweeds came striding into the post office; none, at any rate, that he wanted to look at.

The fascination of the electoral register waned. He went along to the newsagent's to buy papers. He picked out two dailies and asked for a copy of the *Round Table*. The man behind the counter gave him an odd look. If he didn't actually sniff, there was a sniff in his attitude. Peter frowned. A nice state of things when a patriot was something to be sniffed at! For two pins he'd send a subscription to Miss Dubetat to help the youth movement.

He saw with some interest that he had bought a new issue of the *Round Table*, on sale that day. He folded it carefully and put it in a pocket, out of sight. He carried the other papers openly, and went on along the High Street, still with an eye on the cars.

When he reached the church at the end of the street, the attractions of Bosverran were exhausted. There was nothing to do except have a drink at one of the pubs. He hesitated. He was a little tired of the gloom-laden landlord of the Green Dragon. At the door of the Commercial he hesitated, remembering Mr. Murrison's casual invitation to him for that morning. If he entered, he might have to drink with the man. "Alfie and I will be here." No time had been stated. They might have been in and gone. They might not be coming at all. Anyway, he would risk it.

He opened the door of the bar and went inside. Murrison and Alfie were in the far corner. The huge man, the Falstaff with the baby face and the china blue eyes, overlapped a wheel-back chair. The small, jockey-like valet sat perched on the edge of the wall bench, craning forward, his thin body bent as if he were riding a race. Except for the landlord, they had the place to themselves.

Peter was so sure that he would appear to be keeping the appointment made the previous night that he walked straight to Murrison. The result was surprising. Instead of hailing him with his usual *bon homie,* Murrison paid no attention at all. He sat balanced on his chair in an attitude of sagging exhaustion, staring hopelessly at the wall in front of him. After a moment, Alfie looked round and scowled.

Peter said "Good-morning."

This was not successful, so he added, "I thought I *would* drop in."

The stress was intended to recall the fat man's invitation, but the words seemed to have no meaning for him. Only the sound of being addressed penetrated. He turned slowly and gazed at Peter, but the china blue eyes were like blind eyes, insensitive to light.

"It's your friend," Alfie snarled at him. "Wake up, guv! Wake up, can't you?"

He grasped one massive knee and shook it, and something began to move under the flesh. The eyes saw, but they were dull in seeing. The reedy voice was thin and dry.

"Mr. Ackland . . . Good-morning."

From no expression at all, the eyes awakened to a dazed apprehension, peering through a fog. The words had taken a great effort. He tried to say more.

"What can . . . ? What?"

"Take it easy, guv," Alfie interjected sharply. "Just sit back while I buy a drink." Rising, he snapped resentfully at Peter: "Beer, isn't it?"

Peter wanted to refuse, but Alfie crossed to the bar without waiting for an answer.

"Two pints and a double Scotch," the man ordered.

There was a tumbler instead of the usual mead goblet in front of Murrison.

The fat man shook his head and blinked. He pressed the lids tightly over his eyes, screwing up and pleating the rolls of flesh till his face was a grotesque picture of agony. When he opened his eyes, he had made some little recovery.

"I must apologise," he said. "Ap-pologise."

The stupefied, dazed look was gone from him, but his voice seemed unsure.

Peter stared. "It's all right," he said. "You don't have to apologise. I merely looked in."

"Not all right. Unpardonable ... I invited you. Here I am. What are you going to drink?"

"I think your man has ordered."

"My man? My faithful man. He's looking after you, is he? He's good at that. Unfortunately I'm not at my best. You understand? I had a bad night, very bad. My faithful man will tell you. The attack came on soon after I got to my room, and the fool was not there to help me. If he'd given me ephedrine at once . . . you understand? But he was snoring in his room. You know what it's like? You can't breathe. You fight, you struggle, you feel you're going to choke to death. Then the coughing. . . ."

One fat hand made a gesture. The blue eyes were quite sentient now, pleading earnestly, curiously urgent. Curiously frightened, too, as if the asthmatic expected another attack at any moment.

"It went on for hours, Mr. Ackland. It was long after cockcrow before I got to sleep. Of course, my faithful man was with me by that time. He's like a policeman: always shows up after the event."

Alfie came hurrying with the drinks. He slapped down a whisky tumbler in front of Murrison and shoved a pint of bitter at Peter.

"What's he been telling you, Mr. Ackland?" he asked curtly.

Murrison laughed, but there was no enjoyment in the laugh and his foot failed to do its customary tap-dance.

"What have I been telling you, Mr. Ackland?" he said, in a faint parody of the valet. "Is it any business of yours?" he demanded of the man with sudden violence. "Do I have to get your permission to talk about my asthma? What kind of a damned fool do you think I am? I've been telling him you were up all night with me; how I'd have choked to death ... choked ... "

The vision in his mind made him catch his breath. Fear leaped to his eyes, and his hand went to his collar and fumbled with it, loosening it.

Alfie clamped a hand on his master's shoulder and pushed him back in his chair.

"Take it easy," he said, with more menace than plea in his voice. "You know what happens when you get excited. You know what happens. Just sit back and rest. That's all."

"Don't give me orders, you little swine! I know what to do."

"Okay! You know what to do."

Alfie turned his back and went to the counter to pick up his beer and his change. Murrison watched him, and the look on his face reminded Peter of the moment when the fat man had grasped the cat and hurled it at that other bar-counter.

Peter could understand a distaste for Alfie. At the best of times there was something highly disagreeable about the little man; and now was not the best of times. But there was more to the present situation than mere distaste. Peter felt embarrassed. He was an intruder, an interloper. He felt that Murrison resented his presence nearly as much as Alfie so evidently did. He wanted to go. Riding with Murrison in the car yesterday, he had had fantastic fears of abduction, of robbery with violence. He had upbraided himself, blaming his state of mind. The thought that these two could be dangerous had seemed preposterous. Now he was not so sure that he had been right in dismissing the idea as fanciful. There *was* something frightening about the two men, and the less he had to do with them, the better.

He made uncertain noises in his throat. He said: "I'm afraid I butted in on you. I'll be getting on my way."

Murrison wasn't listening. He seemed to have forgotten Peter's existence. He lifted the tumbler, and his hand shook so much, he put it down again. He tried again a moment later, got the glass to his mouth and poured in the neat whisky. Then his great body was sagging again, overlapping the seat of the chair, and he stared at the wall with glazed, unseeing eyes. He was remote, withdrawn into some queer state of hypnosis.

Alfie returned with his beer and stood in front of Murrison, looking down at him. He frowned. He didn't approve at all. When he shifted his gaze, he found Peter staring at him.

He said, as if that was that: "He told you, didn't he? He had a bad night."

"Looks to me as if he's had too much whisky too early," Peter answered. "Is that good for his asthma?"

Alfie stared. There was a lot in the stare, but nothing good.

"You don't have to worry about his asthma," Alfie said. "You just worry about yourself."

"A good idea," Peter agreed. "I'll start at once. I always do my worrying in the open air."

He was on his feet as he spoke. He pushed a chair out of his way and it toppled. A crash would be too much of an effect for an exit. He shot out a hand to steady the chair and knocked over his untouched glass of bitter. The beer swilled over the table, cascaded, trickled. He watched one stream of it flow away from him till it met the barrier of a fat forearm in the sleeve of a sports jacket. Automatically, Peter reached for the empty glass and stood it up. The fat sleeve soaked up the beer, but Murrison made no move, and his man took no notice. The jockey was riding his race again, leaning forward in a Tod Sloan crouch.

The landlord lifted the flap and came through the slot in the counter with a cloth.

Peter wanted to laugh. He was also shaking with anger; not at Murrison or Alfie, it seemed to him, but at the perversity of the inanimate; the chair, the table, the glass. His rage was a flood, submerging reason. Before it overcame him, he had meant to say a word of apology to the landlord for his clumsiness. Now he had a desire to hurl the other glasses to the floor, and the table with them. Instead, he walked out. He let the door slam behind him and fled along the High Street, in a sort of haze. He was not conscious of seeing anything till the skytip near Braddock's house lifted its enormous cone before him.

Then he was aware that his breathing was becoming laboured. He had been walking very rapidly and now he slowed down to his customary pace. He had put quite some distance between himself and Mr. Murrison, but his humiliation had come with him. He blamed Braddock. If it hadn't been for Braddock, he would never have encountered Murrison and his incredible valet, would never have been involved in that undignified scene. He felt like telling Braddock just what he thought of him. In the absence of the fellow, he could only look with acute displeasure on his place of residence.

That house was just the awkward, thrown-up sort of thing you might associate with the man. It was sloppy, untidy, bad in detail. Everything was wrong. And there was that offensive overflow pipe, projecting over the approach to the door.

Peter glanced at it disdainfully as he passed. He glanced at it a second time, and halted. He thought he saw water dripping from it. He moved closer to make sure that it wasn't coming from the guttering above. After all the rain in the night a blocked gutter might still be brimming over. But there was nothing wrong with the gutter. The drip was from the wastepipe, an overflow from the supply cistern inside the house.

He had known it would happen as soon as Braddock's back was turned.

Drip . . . drip . . . drip. . . .

Slowly. The drops formed very slowly. They fell straight and splashed on the path. In a wind they would be blown against the wall. There would be more green lichen on the wall by the time Braddock returned.

Peter shrugged. It was no concern of his. He was not Braddock's plumber. The damned thing could go on dripping till doomsday for all he cared. He shrugged again, and went on his way.

There were two letters on the mat the next morning.

Standing in the untidy hall, Peter felt in his pocket for a pen. No pen, no pencil. Forgetting pen or pencil was one of his habitual sins. He had started this bright day in tip-top form, feeling well. Now, because he had no pencil to redirect Braddock's confounded mail, he felt the nervous irritation rising in him again, Instead of dropping these letters in the pillar-box at the top of the High Street, he would have to return to the farm. It was true he might use pen or pencil at the post office, but he wanted to keep out of Bosverran, wanted to avoid another meeting with Murrison. Then he had the obvious thought. In all that mess on the kitchen table, there might be a pen or pencil. He had seen a bottle of ink somewhere. He tried to remember where.

Drip . . . drip . . . drip. . . .

It was the water from the overflow pipe.

The day was very still, the house very silent.

He moved towards the kitchen. He took a couple of steps, then halted, shocked by a noise. He wheeled, nerves jangling. The front door had closed with a crash, as if it had been jerked from the outside.

No doubt it was merely the state of his nerves that suggested he was a prisoner in the house. He had left the key in the lock, and someone had turned it on him.

Absurd! He told himself it was nonsense, yet, with the crash of the door, the house filled with menace. There was danger, the more frightening because it was without reason and from an unknown source.

After the first moment of paralysis, he insisted that he was being absurd. For one thing, the key did not lock the door. It was used merely to draw back the latch of the old-fashioned spring mechanism.

He went back and turned the knob. There was no resistance, no sinister figure waiting for him beyond the threshold. He removed the key, swung the door back, and watched it. It began to close very slowly; suddenly it developed impetus, and shut with a crash.

A very simple explanation, but it did not dispose of the feeling of menace. Somehow the danger was still there.

He went to the kitchen, and was not surprised to find it in a worse state than before. Braddock certainly must have made a frantic search for something before his departure, because here, as in the hall, drawers had been left open and things strewn over the floor in fantastic disorder.

Peter found pen and ink on the table. He pushed the soldering-iron out of his way, brushed some solder splashes aside, then discovered that he had left the slip of paper bearing Braddock's address in another jacket.

He curbed a fresh wave of irritation He remembered Pero's Hotel. He tried to recall the street. Somewhere in W.C.2.

Drip . . . drip . . . drip. . . .

When you were inside the house, the falling water had a different sound. It thudded on the path as if there were a hollow under the paving. It seemed to be falling a little faster now.

Thud . . . thud . . . thud. . . .

Gladdon Street!

He wrote the London address on the two envelopes.

He went out of the house, closed the door, then tested it to make sure that the spring lock had secured it. He eyed the overflow pipe warily and stepped off the path to avoid a falling drop.

On the way back from the post box, he looked again at the dripping pipe. He shrugged his shoulders and went on, but he could not shrug the thing out of his mind. Down the slope to the farm, he seemed to stride to the rhythm of the drip. It worried him while he read the news in the Tregethneys' papers. It was only when he became absorbed in a book that he managed to forget it. The book took him away from himself and the problems of living. He was at peace, feeling very well indeed, when Mrs. Tregethney called him to lunch. He felt even better when he saw the enormous Cornish pasty confronting him. He had an appetite to cope with it. Cornwall was beginning to have a restorative effect. The doctor had been right. He owed him a vote of thanks for sending him to this –

Plink . . . plink . . . plink. . . .

He tried to ignore it, but it would not be ignored. The room in which he had his meals was next to the kitchen, and Mrs. Tregethney had left the door open. There was a tin tray or baking dish or something in the sink, and the kitchen tap was dripping.

Plink . . . plink . . . plink. . . .

The same rhythm. Almost exactly.

He called: "Mrs. Tregethney, would you mind turning the tap off?"

"My dear life, yes!"

He heard her scurry to the sink. Then she came to the doorway. "I'm sorry," she said. "I didn't notice. We don't aim to waste water like that in these parts. There's always a shortage, no matter how it rains, and the council is always nagging us to save. Half summer they make you feel it's a crime to take a bath. Here we live in the wettest country on earth, and there's never any water. It doesn't make sense, does it?"

"No, it doesn't."

There was silence in the kitchen till he was served with apple pie and cream. Then there came a clatter of plates in the sink, and he listened, expecting the sequel, almost fearful of it.

Plack. . . plack . . . plack. . . .

Now there was a dinner-plate under the tap instead of a tin tray, but for him the drops of water were falling on the garden path at Braddock's place. The sound reproached him, nagging him as a town councillor might nag. It was disgraceful. It should be stopped. Hurriedly, he finished his lunch and went to his room, but he still heard the dripping of water. After a while, he left the house and walked to the big clay pit in search of Captain Hicks. And the sound followed him. It was torture by water. He was held beneath the overflow pipe and the drops hammered him, boring into him. There was only one way to escape.

He felt in his pocket to make sure he had Braddock's key. Abruptly he changed his course, turning towards the house. Perhaps the ball-cock that supplied the cistern needed an adjustment to make the float work properly. It was a simple piece of mechanism, and probably he could fix it without much difficulty. Or turn the water off at the main, perhaps. At any rate, he would have a look at it before he called in a plumber.

Chapter 6

HE had never been upstairs in the house, but he was incurious about the lay-out. He knew the bathroom must be at the end of the landing on the southern side, and was fairly certain that the water cistern must be somewhere near the bathroom. He was right. Part of the cistern was actually in the bathroom, for the bottom of it came down through the timbered ceiling. It was a galvanised tank, about three feet by two, and he judged it would be little more than three feet in depth, which meant that there would be two feet of it above the ceiling. A covered man-hole alongside was evidently intended to give access to the top part.

Peter heard the faint hiss of running water as he contemplated the clumsy job. When he stood on the bathroom chair he could lift up the hinged trap of the man-hole. He could see the top of the cistern a few inches below the slope of the roof, but he would need to be higher to reach it.

A small table at the other end of the landing looked sturdy enough to bear his weight. As he went to get it, he caught a glimpse, through a partly open door, of what was evidently Braddock's bedroom. He was not surprised to see signs of the same disorder he had observed downstairs. Drawers of a tallboy and dressing-table had been pulled out. Things had been dropped on the floor. Such determined untidiness was really preposterous. It was a wonder that Braddock managed to keep the services of the woman who came in to clean for him. Of course, he had packed up in a great hurry, but even so. . . .

Peter dismissed it. It was no business of his. He carried the table to the bathroom, placed the chair on it, and clambered up. Above the waist he was through the man-hole, and he had to dip his head to avoid a rafter. The dusty place seemed crowded with the dim shapes of timbers. No doubt there was room for a crouching man in the cramped space above the manhole, but he had no reason to test it, for he could reach the business part of the cistern. He removed the wooden cover and groped with one hand.

There was a dim light under the roof, a murky penetration between the slats of a ventilating louvre in the northern wall. It was too dim to show him the inside of the cistern, so he struck a match and took a look at the ball-float at the end of its thin metal arm. The escaping water whispered, but there wasn't enough of it to cause a ripple. He depressed the copper ball, and the sibilant complaint of the water leaped to a sharp hissing. He raised the ball a fraction of an inch, and the flow stopped. He could tell from the feel of it when depressed that there was no puncture in the ball. It looked as if the cause of the trouble was a worn valve. When he allowed the ball to fall back in the water the slight flow started again. He could stop it temporarily by tying the arm of the ball to a rafter. Then Braddock could get the valve fixed when he returned.

Peter struck another match to examine the rafter, and found a nail that would serve his purpose. Then, as the match was dying, he looked down at the arm of the ball and saw a loop of cord over it. Perhaps on some past occasion the arm had been tied up to keep the valve closed.

The red-glowing end of the match fell into the water. Peter felt along the arm for the cord, found it, and tried to draw the end of it out of the water. He gave it a tug, but it still resisted. Then he realised that here was the trouble. The cord, caught somehow at the bottom of the tank, was applying just enough tension to the arm of the valve lever to prevent a complete closure.

It was good, stout window-blind cord. The loop round the metal arm of the ball-cock was loose, but the knot had been tied tightly and contraction of the wet cord had tightened it. Peter tried hard to undo the knot but it stubbornly refused to yield. He tried to get both hands to the job, but the cramped space under the sloping roof made this impossible for one standing halfway through the man-hole. He might have managed it by climbing up through the man-hole and squeezing round to the other side of the tank, but he'd be damned if he was going to do that. He had made himself filthy enough already. All he could do now was fish out his pen-knife and cut the cord.

He did it. An effort to hold the cord failed. It slipped away and fell into the water, but he saw nothing to bother about in this. He had stopped the drip from the overflow pipe, and that, he told himself, was all that mattered. The rest was Braddock's funeral. He was pleased with himself. The drip had worried him and he had stopped it. If he had a house like this, he would have it running smoothly in a week. But heaven forbid that he should ever have a house like this.

He covered the cistern, got down from the chair onto the table, then reached up to close the man-hole. As the trap fell into position, a thud shook the house, but it was not caused by the trap. It came from below. It must be that confounded front door slamming. But, if he had left it open on entering, why had it taken so long to slam? And had he left it open? He had taken the key out of the lock. He had it in his pocket now.

He got down from the table slowly, listening. He put the chair back in position, silently, still listening.

Nothing. The house was very quiet.

He lifted the table to take it back to the landing, but lowered it at once and listened again. This time he heard sounds: footsteps and the opening of a room door.

Braddock must have returned sooner than expected. No one else would have a key. No one else would have the right to enter.

He was on the point of calling out when he heard more footsteps. They were not Braddock's. He listened intently, his nerves tightening again. Now he would have to face an interloper, a thief perhaps.

More sounds came up to him. Quick footsteps on the stone floor of the kitchen; not like a man's at all. A woman's, then? The cleaning woman had no key; Braddock wouldn't have her in the house unless he were at home.

Peter moved to the landing, and looked down. He had a positive feeling that the intruder intended to come upstairs. His heart pounding, he waited. Then he saw the top of her head. Glancing up as she began to mount she saw him, and halted as if she had been hit.

She was the dark girl he had seen in Bosverran, the glamorous vestal of *Excalibur*, the beauty of the League of Patriots.

If Peter Ackland was staggered, the girl was completely unnerved. The fear in her eyes would have set the whole Round Table spurring to the rescue. She was a damsel who looked very appealing in distress, and what knight could have withheld protection and comfort from such frightened loveliness?

Well, Sir Peter Ackland for one.

The somewhat imperfect knight spoke sharply and ungallantly from the landing.

"What are you doing in this house?"

Surprise, nervousness, unbroken inhibitions, the divorce from his wife – all put an edge to his voice. The girl looked up at him and her dark eyes seemed to expand. She had opened her mouth, perhaps to yell, and it was still open. She tried to make it move, but it wouldn't. She seemed to be the victim of lockjaw, doomed to the perpetual presentation of a frozen scream, a picture without a sound-track, but not entirely without motion. One rather beautiful hand grabbed at the banister for support.

In the face of her dismay, the imperfect knight gained courage. He had affirmed and reaffirmed to himself that he didn't like this girl; that he detested the feminine attitude he felt sure she epitomised. Now, here was the confirmation he needed; here was arrogance indeed! Snooping in other people's houses! But for what purpose, in heaven's name? Was she going to plead feminine curiosity? Probably. But she wasn't going to get far by turning those big eyes on him. She should answer him. He would have the truth.

"What's the idea?"

There was possibly a falling off in incisiveness, a descent from that upper-floor dignity to a cellarage of colloquialism. The girl seemed to take courage. At least she recovered the power of speech.

"The door was open, so I walked in." Her voice was low, with a nice husky note. It was tremulous, but that was doubtless assumed. "I called was there anyone home, and no one answered, so I thought you were out for a minute or two since the door was open, and – well, it occurred to me I might just as well have a look round."

"May I know the reason why you walk in and have a look round?"

"Do you have to stand up there, shouting down at me?" She had the effrontery to scowl at him, as if he were the offender. "It seems to me that this is a little peculiar to say the least. I was told I could come out here any afternoon. I didn't expect you'd be waiting at the top of the stairs to pounce on me. You – you scared the life out of me."

"I was not waiting to pounce on you." Peter put a sharp, indignant protest into the words. He descended the stairs, although he had the feeling that he was weakening his position by that act, since it was, in effect, an admission that he shouldn't be standing up there shouting down at her. She was over the first shock of the meeting and seemed to be full of assurance, as if she had a right to walk into the house. But he was not going to have her challenging him or his behaviour. He would be cool, but quite ruthless.

"What can I do for you?"

It had all the coolness of a shoe salesman on commission.

"Why," she said, with a forgiving smile, "I came out to see the house. From what the agent in Truro told me, it sounded just the sort of thing I was looking for. I'm not so sure, now that I see the place. It is a bit isolated, isn't it? What date would you be prepared to vacate?"

Peter blinked. "Wait a minute! You say a house-agent in Truro gave you this address?"

"Certainly. Mr. Pengelley."

"He told you the house is for sale?"

"Not for sale. To be let, furnished. He gave me an order to view." She opened her handbag and went through it. She went through it a second time. "Oh, dear!" she said. "I must have left it at the guest house. I was asking the landlady how I could find the place. I'm a stranger here."

"Are you? And you want to live here?"

"Just for a few months. I think it's so much nicer to have a place of your own, don't you? Especially when a woman friend's ready to share with you. Have you got an electric cooker?"

"The place doesn't belong to me. I didn't know it was to be let, either. You'd better see Mr. Braddock when he gets back. He's away in London for a few days."

The girl appeared puzzled. "Mr. Braddock? Who's Mr. Braddock?"

"He's the tenant."

"I don't understand. Are you Mr. Forbes?"

It was Peter's turn to be puzzled. "Who's Mr. Forbes?"

"Mr. Forbes is the man I had to see." She stared. "Wait a minute. This is Bosveor Cottage, isn't it?"

"I believe it's known as Trevone. You seem to have come to the wrong place."

"Oh, dear!" Her accent was of acute dismay. "That landlady of mine misdirected me. No wonder you were angry. I thought I was expected. That's why I walked in and called out. I don't know how to apologise. Do you know where this Bosveor Cottage is?"

"Haven't an idea. You'd better ask somebody local."

"Are you staying here while Mr. Braddock's away?"

"Not at all. I just looked in to fix a leak in the water system. No, I'm not the plumber," he added hastily. "I'm just . . ."

"Keeping an eye on things for him? Did he leave in a hurry? The place is awfully untidy, isn't it?"

"That has nothing to do with me." Severity returned to him. The implication was that it had nothing to do with her, either.

"Sorry." The girl smiled. "It was impertinent of me, wasn't it? I'd better leave you to your repairs."

"I've finished, thank you. I'm locking up. If you want to know about the Forbes place, they can probably tell you at the farm down the lane. The Tregethneys know all the local people. I'm staying with them."

"Are you? I don't think I'll bother any more to-day. The walk from Bosverran was longer than I expected."

He was close to her, observing her closely. He had the impression then that she was frightened; that all her assurance was just a pretence.

But this, he argued, was absurd. There was nothing to frighten her except himself, and, even in his worst moments, he was scarcely an object of fear. Perhaps she was just shy, nervous of strangers, and her mistake about the house had upset her.

Moving towards the front door, she glanced back at him, and he thought he detected a tremor in her lips. He felt that he might relax a little, say something that would show her that she had nothing to worry about, but he couldn't think of the right thing to say. They went out into the garden and he slammed the door behind him, then tried it to make sure that the spring lock had worked. The girl seemed to be in a hurry. She reached the gate to the roadway a few paces ahead of him, but he caught her up. She looked hurriedly along the road in the direction of the skytip, then turned to him.

"I'm sorry I disturbed you," she told him. "You must have thought I was very rude."

He ignored it. With the mild sun lighting up her clear skin, he thought she was quite lovely. He said: "Didn't I see you at a meeting of the League of Patriots in London a few weeks back?"

She hesitated. He feared she was going to deny it, and he didn't like the idea that she might lie to him, especially as she could have no cause to lie.

"Yes," she answered. "Possibly you did."

He had a preposterous desire to invite her to afternoon tea at the farm.

She said: "I work for Mr. Britt. That's why I want a cottage in Cornwall."

On the face of it, there seemed to be no connection, but the Arthurian tradition might provide some esoteric link. Camelford, the reputed Camelot, was not far away, and beyond were Tintagel and Merlin's cave.

The girl said hastily: "I must go now. Good-bye, Mr. Ackland."

"Good-bye."

She walked rapidly away, leaving him in a tangle of myth and legend, a little bemused. He observed her easy, athletic stride as she followed the curve of the road round the base of the skytip. Few people walked attractively. She did. There was beauty in the movement of her body, beauty in everything she did.

Watching her, he felt a twinge of loneliness. It became less tolerable with each step that she took away from him; and he had let her go, had made no effort to hold her. Tomorrow she would set out again to look for the man Forbes and his Bosveor Cottage, and he might have offered her his help.

It was not too late. If he hurried, he could overtake her. To-night he would find out from the Tregethneys where Forbes lived. Tomorrow he would meet her and take her to the place. Not that he intended anything more than a friendly gesture. He couldn't do less, really. If he let her go now, he might never have another opportunity of talking to her, and he did want to make that friendly gesture.

He hurried along the road after her. If she looked back he would wave, signal to her to wait for him. But she never turned; was never conscious that he was following her. For a moment or two she was hidden from him by the cone of the skytip. He ran till he came round the curve of the road and saw her again. There was a stationary car just ahead of her, and he recognised it at once as the battered Austin Twelve used by Mr. Murrison and his valet. He hadn't heard the engine, but it was possible that Alfie had been coasting down the road from the clay pits that came round the other side of the mound, and the gallant Mr. Murrison, spotting the wayfarer, had bade his chauffeur pull up.

As if to confirm this view, the car decanted the fat man into the roadway, and he waddled along a few yards to meet the girl. He seemed to have recovered from his indisposition of the morning, but possibly he was not at the top of his form. He gestured towards the car, but the girl seemed unwilling to accept a lift. They talked, standing in the middle of the road. Murrison repeated his gesture towards the car, and the girl decided to ride with him.

A moment later the car was rolling down the hill, and Peter Ackland gazed after it till there was nothing to see but a trail of white dust.

He felt cheated and, suddenly, depressed.

Chapter 7

He continued to feel depressed, and resented the fact.

He had no wish to think about the girl, yet he went on thinking about her. He thought of her as a singular type, or singular, perhaps, in certain attributes. Or in the grouping of attributes. He had to be precise in analysis in order to be fair. She had a lot of youthful self-assurance, but there was time for her to grow out of that. She was inclined to adopt an air of superiority, but that might be the result of her political associations. All these idealists had a tendency to look down on those to whom they wished to give the keys of the kingdom.

But there was no harm in this, so far as he could see. Certainly there was no harm in the girl's association with the cause of Arthur Lamorak-Britt. There might be aspects of the National League of Patriots that invited ridicule, that roused people to impatient criticism if not downright antagonism. All this romantic stuff, this Arthurian fustian, was a bit silly, but the movement professed aims that seemed fundamentally sound, aims that appealed to the ordinary man who was tired of the old political dog-fight. In this time of dreadful impasse, Arthur Lamorak-Britt was stirring people from their apathy, showing them a feasible path, making them think. Especially people with no special interest in politics; intelligent people like Peter Ackland.

Stirred from his apathy, Peter sat down after supper with the new number of the *Round Table* in hand. Before his encounter with the dark girl in Braddock's house, he had merely glanced at it. A shameful neglect, no doubt. The menace of apathy was ever in one's path, a trap, a stagnant pool deeper than Dozmare on Bodmin Moor, into which

Sir Bedevere threw *Excalibur*, unless he threw it into Looe Pool.

Once more the grave, searching eyes of Arthur Lamorak-Britt challenged the reader from the printed page. Here was a new pose, a new aspect of the leader. You saw him as a soul in pain, the noble brow wrinkled carefully, the heavy actor's countenance sicklied o'er with the pale cast of thought. A natural for Hamlet, the troubled prince meditating on the decadence of a State. You had only to look at him to know that he was thinking for you, that his agony was your agony; more composed, perhaps, but still yours.

Peter turned the page. He was growing a little tired of Mr. Britt. He wanted to find out how Primrose Dubetat was doing. He turned another page. There was no picture of Miss Dubetat, but she had space in her usual corner, and was doing nicely. Three new youth clubs had been formed, and up and down the country the young patriots were flourishing, holding parties, picnics, jumble sales.

Miss Dubetat, however, had an arch way of writing that Peter found nauseating. It was difficult to relate that style to the creature of dark-eyed beauty, but there it was, and it confirmed his first and harshest judgment of her. She was not a rational mind attracted by the sound planks in Mr. Britt's political platform; she was merely an empty-headed female who yearned over the romantic flummery; yearned, most likely, for the great hero himself. No doubt she kept *Idylls of the King* beside her bed, and pinned up those expensive half-tones from the *Round Table,* Depression deepened. To hell with Miss Dubetat.

He turned away from the corner of the youth clubs, but the dark girl would not leave him alone. Her image came between him and the pages. Words might filter through the filmy ghost of her, but not the sense of them. Only one item held him, and much of that was apprehended but vaguely. Something about a gauntlet thrown down, a challenge to be taken up, slanderous attacks that could no longer be brooked, vile insinuations, malicious innuendos. Then the last line, the kernel of the nut, stood out more sharply:

In consequence of this, solicitors have been instructed to issue a writ of libel against the Sunday Gazette.

So Mr. Britt had decided to take notice of the constant enemy, to fight back. The *Gazette* had long been accustomed to pour scorn on Britt and the Patriots, to impute totalitarian designs, to hint at a nice bit of nest feathering. Possibly it had gone on to more reckless charges, and at last committed itself to something actionable. Peter did not know. The *Gazette* was not a paper he read. He hadn't seen a copy for weeks. He was curious for a moment, but not moved to seek further information. He saw nothing of peculiar interest in the matter. There was no reason why he should link it up with Henry Braddock. It was without significance for him, something seen in print through the dissolving vision of a girl. He was still walking in the dark, with no awareness of the danger into which his innocence was leading him. He was not even aware of the dark.

He threw the *Round Table* aside, stretched, drank his glass of milk, and went to bed.

In his innocence, he slept quite soundly.

There was one letter for Braddock in the morning. It lay face down on the mat and, as Peter picked it up, he saw the imprint on the back of the envelope. He blinked and read it a second time. The *Sunday Gazette*.

Curious. Rather a coincidence, the *Gazette's* popping up like this in Braddock's house, when only last night he had been reading about that writ for libel.

He shrugged. Why should he think it curious? Did he imagine it linked Braddock with the threatened libel action? Braddock had probably been trying to sell them an article on the future of Albania or the Pan-Latvian movement. Or possibly he knew someone on the staff.

Peter pencilled the address of Pero's Hotel on the letter and put it in his pocket. He was about to slam the front door, and go on his way to the pillar-box when he remembered he had left the table from the landing in the bathroom. He went back inside the house and closed the front door.

Curious. The comment was in his mind a second time, and he stood on the mat, arrested by a thought. He had closed the door automatically, and in that moment he was sure he had closed it the same way the previous day. The spring latch was fast. From the outside only a key could operate it.

"The door was open, so I walked in."

An echo of the girl's voice contradicted him; the low, husky, persuasive voice.

Well, possibly, but he could have sworn. . . .

He went upstairs to the bathroom. He listened intently. There was not a whisper of sound from the cistern, so that was all right. He carried the table back to the landing, and once more, as he passed, he caught a glimpse of the bedroom, once more the litter on the floor impressed him as ridiculous. Not in any urgency of packing, not in the most frantic last-minute search for something mislaid, was there any reason or excuse for it. Really –

A thought came to him like a sudden drum-beat, halting him in his stride. He put down the table with a crash.

He pushed the door wide open and entered the bedroom. The percussive thought was confirmed in the first glance, confirmed beyond all doubt. The place had been searched. Then, as he stared at the chaos around him, he knew he had not been wrong about Braddock's fear, not wrong about the bulging pocket. Everything that had happened since his first meeting with the man took on a sinister colour. All that he saw meant danger, but the threat was to another man. He could not yet see that he might be in peril. His own reaction was of anger. He was angry with Braddock because the man had involved him in some questionable affair without warning him. For two pins he would slam the door of the bedroom, walk out of the house, and send the key to Pero's Hotel with a note recommending Braddock to go to the devil.

The man was a spy, perhaps, in the pay of a foreign power. He had attracted the attention of other shabby agents, national or international. He had something they wanted to get hold of, some valuable information, some secret plan.

Peter knew the tricks of the miserable trade. He had read all about them in numerous works of fiction. The fact that the tenant of Trevone

Cottage had been living the life of a recluse, with no opportunity to prepare anything more secret or valuable than a ground plan of Bosverran, did not halt his theorising. Braddock was the master-spy, with agents to serve him in all the vulnerable centres. When necessary, he went to London to confer with the members of his ring. His enemies knew this very well. They had waited and watched. They had seen him board the train at Par. Then they had come here in the night, to ransack the house.

The bedroom certainly afforded a convincing example of a room ransacked. The bed had been stripped, the ticking of the overlay had been slashed open, the box spring had been similarly treated, the pillows had been ripped up, the carpet rolled back, a flooring-board lifted. Not a point in the routine of the well-trained spy had been neglected.

It was the same in the other rooms – in the study, in the spare bedroom, in the living-room downstairs. Peter went through the house, his nerves jangling, his thoughts racing. The very thoroughness of the mess suggested that the searchers must have failed, because they had not stopped until everything had been disturbed, and it was scarcely conceivable that they had come upon their objective in the last cushion or behind the final picture.

The study represented the peak of their performance. Braddock had collected a number of books, and they had been taken from the shelves, examined, and tossed aside. The litter of papers on and near the desk was formidable. All papers, wherever found, had been closely inspected, or so it seemed, and it was, therefore, a. reasonable deduction that some writing, some letter, deed, document, plan, something on paper had been the objective.

Peter stared down at the desk, at the portable typewriter almost snowed under. A batch of newspaper cuttings hung precariously over the side of an open drawer. He saw the name of Britt in a headline, and it stayed in his mind.

When he had completed a swift survey of the ground-floor rooms, he went back upstairs to the study to look at the cuttings. They were from the *Sunday Gazette,* the series of attacks on the National League of Patriots that had finally spurred Britt to take legal action. They had lively and pointed headlines. The articles were racy in style but very direct, and what wasn't expressed, you could read between the lines. As they went on, there was little need to read between the lines. The *Gazette* was carrying on a full-scale war against the N.L.P. and trying, deliberately it seemed, to provoke the libel action which now threatened.

Britt was a fascist, a racketeer. Before the war he had been associated with one of the fascist groups in the pay of Hitler. He might cry out that he had been deceived, that he had resigned in abhorrence, but where was the fascist that really changed his spots? The N.L.P. was just the old dreary brand of totalitarianism dressed up in a patched cloak of romantic rhapsody, a mantle of Mabinogion moonshine, and it didn't need radar equipment to detect the familiar viper of anti-Semitism crawling through the Celtic twilight of this junk-shop Joyous Gard.

One article was a scornful analysis of the League's economic proposals, and concluded with the suggestion that the essential operative policy was more booty for Britt. Another article attacked the movement's treasurer, describing him as a maundering Merlin with a wand purloined from the property-room of a provincial pantomime. In the same article a second retainer, dubbed Nordic Nat, came in for brief but scathing attention.

Next, the Youth Department was held up as a feeble effort to imitate the Nazis. The Leader could scarcely countenance Strength through Joy as a slogan, but what was wrong with Power through Popcorn? If the Home Office was diffident about taking notice of the brawls in back alleys that sometimes followed meetings of the N.L.P., it should at least give some attention to the systematic corruption of the young by lemonade and Chelsea buns under the direction of Aunt Primrose.

Peter, who had been running quickly down the columns of print, halted and reread this last part more carefully. Other comments had seemed to him unfair, because full of a purposeful malice that seemed to have some twist of jealousy or personal venom behind it, but yet amusing. What followed was outrageous in his view, for here it was implied, quite subtly but inescapably, that the disparity in years between Aunt Primrose and her charges must make it difficult for her to appreciate their real needs, even though it might be argued, in the case of some ladies, that age could not wither nor custom stale their infinite resource.

Undoubtedly the picture conveyed was of some elderly fusspot whose only approach to childhood must be through her senile fantasies. Peter, with all sorts of facts and deductions milling round in his head, was bewildered by this new statement. The dark girl could not be much more than twenty-four, if that. Certainly she was of an age to sympathise with the needs of youth, since they were her own needs. The article was rubbish, a malevolent distortion, a disgrace. Not that the girl meant anything to him. It was the principle of the thing that made him furious.

He read on and finally came to the story that had provoked Britt to action. The date of two Sundays ago was on the top of it, and that same date had been mentioned in the news of the impending suit. It was a short article. It gave what was described as the known or stated details of Britt's war-time record and challenged him to answer a series of questions.

The known details followed a familiar pattern of gallantry and misfortune. Britt had offered himself promptly enough as a candidate for the Royal Air Force. He had qualified as a pilot officer. He had taken part in hazardous missions, had chalked up some good performances, but a raid over Cologne had put an end to this particular chapter. With half the crew dead and the bomber on fire, he had had to give the order to bale out. Two of the survivors had evaded capture, but Britt had been taken the moment he touched earth.

What happened after that was his own story, uncorroborated except in a few minor particulars. He had dropped unluckily and injured himself. He had turned up in Stalag Luft so-and-so after an operation and a long period in hospital. Later he had been hurried away for another operation, and, so far as the *Sunday Gazette* could discover, there was no further record of him in any prisoners-of-war camp.

He claimed that he had been sent to East Prussia to receive treatment from a specialist. He was in a critical state, and convalescence was prolonged. Doctors and others had been kind to him, perhaps with a purpose, because presently it had been suggested to him that he could help to bring the war to an end, and at the same time win favoured treatment for himself. He had known what that meant. He had seen enough in the period of his captivity. Frightened youngsters had yielded to the wiles of the Nazis and become traitors to their comrades. But he was no frightened youngster. He was Arthur Lamorak-Britt, and he had rejected all such proposals with scorn and suffered for it. He had been charged with a disciplinary offence and sent to a concentration camp. When the Russians came, the Nazis had fled, and he had escaped. For days he had wandered and at last fallen in with the Americans.

That was the tale according to Britt, and the questions framed by the *Gazette* took the form of a probing cross-examination. What was the nature of the operations on him? Where and when had they been performed? What was the name of the specialist in East Prussia?

Who had proposed to him that he should turn traitor? How much scorn had he poured on the suggestion? What particular form had his scorn taken? What was the nature of his disciplinary offence, the name of the concentration camp, the manner of his escape? If Mr. Britt cared to answer, the columns of the paper were open to him.

The imputation was as clear as if it had been stated boldly in a headline. Britt had worked with the Nazis and knew all their tricks. Unlike the weak-willed dupes who had exposed their own treachery with every move and left a string of witnesses to it in the prisoner-of-war camps, Britt had worked with caution. He had been too astute, too clever to betray himself. He had covered up his tracks with tales of hospitals and rest-homes and concentration camps. Others had tried it, taking assumed names. Others had failed, but Britt had succeeded. That was the charge, and he would have to disprove it. If one piece of incontestable evidence could be brought against him, he would be finished.

Peter dropped the cuttings back in the drawer of the desk and closed it. There was villainy here, and it revolted him. There was villainy either in Britt or in the writer of the articles. The one was arraigned by hint and innuendo. The other was suspect of using a newspaper for the expression of a personal hatred; for that was what the venom in his writing suggested. The writer was out to get Britt, and it seemed a feasible deduction to Peter that the writer was Braddock.

When he thought of *Yugoslavia Tomorrow* he even thought he saw the similarities in style. There were the same angry sarcasms. There was the same devotion to facetious alliteration. Of course, these things were not conclusive, although they might gain a certain weight from material and other factors. This sheaf of cuttings in Braddock's desk, for instance. And the letter from the *Sunday Gazette* now readdressed to Pero's Hotel. Braddock had criticised Britt strongly. Braddock had gone to London expecting to collect some money. From the *Sunday Gazette*? It was possible. The articles were printed under the name of J. Woodforde Bayles, but Braddock was a man of many *noms de guerre* and this might be one of them. It was curious that the *Gazette* should be writing to him in Cornwall, if he had gone to London to get payment for the articles. Curious, but it didn't matter. Peter was determined to have nothing more to do with Braddock. He would 'phone him at Pero's as soon as he could reach the post office. He would tell him that his house had been entered, and searched, and he'd better come home and attend to things, because he, Ackland, was washing his hands of the business.

He shut the front door carefully, then walked rapidly into Bosverran, eager to get Braddock and his affairs out of his mind. He made at once for the post office, dropped the readdressed letter into the box, got the number of Pero's Hotel, and put through a call from one of the 'phone booths. He waited with increasing impatience. He began to think what he would tell Braddock. He had seen no signs of any forcible entry into the house, so a key must have been used. That spring lock on the front door would have presented little difficulty. It was the sort of thing that the expert might open with a strip of celluloid. The job must have been done within a few hours of Braddock's departure; certainly the same night, because the evidence of it had been there in the hall next morning – the oak chest with its lid open, papers, books, articles of clothing scattered on the floor. If he had gone upstairs that morning and seen the state of the bedroom, prompt action could have been taken, but he had been quite unsuspicious. When a man lived in permanent untidiness, you were not likely to take much notice of more disorder in the hall. Anyone might conclude that it was the result of a last minute search for something, and if Braddock had the nerve to complain of neglect or –

"Pero's Hotel." A man's voice crackled in the receiver at his ear.

"Oh, yes. I'd like to speak to Mr. Braddock."

"What name?"

"Braddock. Henry Braddock."

"Just a moment, please."

He waited.

"Hello?"

"Braddock, this is Ackland. I'm glad I caught you in – "

"We have no Mr. Braddock registered with us."

"Not registered?" Peter's voice expressed bewilderment. "He must be. He's staying with you. He went up by the night train on Tuesday. From Cornwall. Hello! Am I speaking to Pero's Hotel?"

"Yes, Pero's. Hold the line a moment."

He held it, gripping the receiver tightly.

The receptionist came back. "I'm sorry, sir. There's no Mr. Braddock here. Is there any message for him, in case he arrives?"

"No. No, thank you. I'll call up again. I'll write."

His words were jerky. The receiver clattered as he returned it to its cradle. He looked round in the act, afraid that someone might be watching him, waiting for him to leave the cabinet. The fear had hit him suddenly while the receptionist was offering to take a message; it had been like a shutter dropping between him and the voice, cutting the transmitted sound to a faint whisper. And through the whisper had come an echo of Braddock's voice, raised against a turbulent background of wind and rain.

"Once I'm on that train, I'll be safe."

Peter stood staring at the telephone. The feeling of sinister things he had had in Braddock's house, of danger surrounding the man, had grown into an apprehension far grimmer. Imagination would no longer be stilled.

"Once I'm on that train...."

But Braddock had been over-confident. His enemies must have found him in London. They were holding him somewhere, because he had something they wanted, something he had picked up in his murky career. They had watched him leave the house, they had entered and searched, and they had failed to find. They had telephoned accomplices in London that the victim was on the night train. And now they had him somewhere and would hold him till he gave in. They would starve him, ill-treat him, beat him up....

That was it all right. They had picked him up at Paddington. Nothing could have happened at this end, because Ben Stevens had driven him to Par. Ben Stevens had probably seen him safely on the train.

Peter darted out a hand to grab the receiver. He couldn't remember the number. He flicked over the pages of the local directory and found it. Stevens wasn't in. He had taken the car to Peake's garage to have something repaired.

Out in the sunlight the whole thing seemed fantastic. There was surely some reasonable explanation. Sunlight, of course, could not dispel the fact that the house had been entered, but it was not to be argued from this that Braddock had been abducted. He might have decided to go to some other hotel. He would call at Pero's for his letters. That must be it. Weren't there cases of people who had lived for years at the Ritz or the Savoy – on paper only?

Ben Stevens was still at Peake's garage. One of the hands pointed him out.

Peter said: "Mr. Stevens? I 'phoned you the other night about a car for Mr. Braddock at Trevone Cottage. Did you see him on the train at Par all right?"

"See him on the train!" Ben Stevens had a loud voice. It roared with careless, almost jovial indignation. "What do you mean, see him on the train? I never seen him at all. I turned out in all that weather, and when I got to the house, it was all dark. I knocked three times, like you said. Then I knocked twenty times off my own bat. No good. The house was empty. Mr. Braddock must have got a lift over to Par, and all I can say is, he might have let me know. If he could get you to call up for a car, he could have got you to cancel it."

Peter stared.

"What's the matter?" Ben Stevens asked. "Anything wrong?"

Peter shook himself. "No. I suppose it's as you say."

"Turning out on a night like that! I waste my petrol, I get wet through, and no fare for my trouble. Who's going to pay me?"

Peter had to shake himself again. He produced a note. "Take it out of that," he said, but Ben Stevens waved the note away.

"Put it back," he roared. "Mr. Braddock's all right. Between you and me, I was only too glad I didn't have to plough a way through to Par."

Peter left the garage with the intention of going straight to the police, but on the way he became doubtful of the course. He questioned his own feeling of alarm for Braddock, questioned all his fears. It wouldn't do to look foolish. He had a need to think things out, to go over everything.

Braddock had made up his mind quite suddenly to leave that night. No one had known about it but Peter and Ben Stevens. Unless someone had overheard the telephone call from the Commercial Hotel. That fellow who had come from the darts' room and waited for the 'phone. He might have heard everything, including the instruction to knock three times. Without the three knocks, Braddock would not have opened the door.

Peter crossed the road to the Commercial and went into the bar. He ordered a drink. He felt he needed it, but a prior need was to look at the situation of the telephone.

He went into the corridor and examined the lay-out. Anyone in the darts' parlour might have heard him, anyone in the bar.

Stepping back through the doorway and seeing his beer on the counter, he had a feeling of repetition. Queer? But of course, it wasn't queer. He was doing exactly what he had done after using the 'phone.

The scene was different. Night had become morning. And there had been customers at the counter, among them Murrison and Alfie.

Thought pulled up with a jerk, and then raced on. Murrison and Alfie had heard him at the telephone. Murrison had thought he had wanted a car for himself, and had said something about offering his own car. And Peter had explained about Braddock.

Good grief! Murrison!

He looked hastily round as though he feared Murrison might have responded to a telepathic invocation. He turned to the landlord. He tried to make his voice sound quite casual.

"Where's our portly friend this morning?"

The landlord looked blank.

"The fat man," Peter explained.

"Mr. Murrison?" The landlord shrugged. "Hasn't been in since yesterday morning. Didn't see him last night. Getting to be a regular, too, him and his man. First night he missed. Gone back to London, I shouldn't wonder. Nice chap. Likes a joke. Jolly. More than you can say for that man of his."

"I thought they might look in."

The landlord shrugged again. "Last I saw of them was yesterday. They left soon after you knocked your beer over."

"What makes you think they've gone back to London?"

"Mr. Murrison said something about packing up. Maybe he meant he'd had enough to drink. I don't know. He was a bit off colour yesterday. Started on Scotch suddenly. Usually sticks to mead."

"I want to find him if he's still here. Do you know where he's been staying?"

"Mrs. Watts, I heard tell. You could try there. It's the last house along Bodmin Terrace from the High Street."

Peter had to know definitely if the fellow had left Bosverran. If he found him at the guest house, he would talk to him about Braddock, watch him closely, try to discover if he knew anything, announce that he was going to the police. It might be inadvisable, all of it, but Peter was in no state of mind for anything but a bull-at-a-gate approach.

If Murrison had departed, he had certainly been in no particular hurry to get away. As late as yesterday afternoon he had had time to stop and offer a lift to a stranger casually encountered on the roadway.

Casual encounter?

Peter put himself under cross-examination as he went along the High Street looking for Bodmin Terrace.

Was it mere coincidence that had brought the Austin to that spot behind the skytip at that particular moment? If Murrison was responsible for the entry and search of Braddock's house, he might have continued to take an interest in the house. Had he gone back to have another look? Had he seen the girl arrive and enter the place? Had he waited for her behind the skytip, believing that she would return that way?

That encounter, that supposed offer of a lift, the talk in the roadway – everything took on a different colour. More than one dialogue could be fitted to the same scene, the same set of gestures. Murrison had waylaid the girl. He had demanded to know why she had gone to the house. He had forced her by threats to enter the car.

Sir Peter Ackland, knight errant, again saw the car speeding along the road to Bosverran, but now it seemed impelled by frantic haste. Had Murrison and his man really abducted that innocent girl, or was he, the witness, going back to the fantastic conception of Murrison he had meditated while himself a passenger in that very car.

Bodmin Terrace! He turned the corner from the High Street. He began to think about the innocent girl. He tried to remember every moment, every speech, every inflection of their clash in Braddock's house. The time sequence was broken up. Words, doubts, fears swung about out of order. Mr. Ackland took over again.

He had accepted the girl's statement that she had found the door open. Now he knew he had closed the door, and the certainty of it shocked him. She had lied to him. She had opened the door with a key.

The sound of her voice came to him, not in husky denial, but in words that betrayed her, the last words she said to him when they parted outside the cottage.

"I must go now. Good-bye, Mr. Ackland."

Mr. Ackland! She had named him, and he had accepted it as a matter of course. Now the significance of her error crashed upon his suspicion-sharpened mind. All her talk about renting a place, about Forbes and Bosveor Cottage, had been invented to get her out of the trap she had walked into. She knew him, she knew all about Braddock and the house she had entered unlawfully. If he had not been there, she would have searched, as someone else had searched before her.

The duplicity of it all appalled him. The thought of her guilt, or the thought of his own gullibility, stopped him in his tracks. Bodmin Terrace. . . . He went on. He was certain now of the result of his mission.

"Mrs. Watts?"

Mrs. Watts was gracious, inviting him in. In his acutely suspicious mood, he believed that this could only mean that there were vacant rooms in the house.

"I believe you have a Mr. Murrison staying with you? Mr. Nathan Murrison?"

"We did have." Mrs. Watts continued to be gracious. "If you want to see him, I'm afraid you're too late. He went back to London last night."

"With his man, I suppose?"

"That's right. In that old car. Him and Mr. Alfie and a young lady."

He felt another shock. "Miss Dubetat?" He pronounced it in two syllables and phonetically.

"I didn't catch her name. She came with them last evening. Mr. Murrison, he'd offered to take her with them to London, and they were in a rare hurry, leaving so unexpectedly I had to rush round and get them something to eat while Mr. Alfie went with the young lady to get her suitcases."

"Oh, dear! I seem to have missed all of them."

Peter judged that a sigh was needed before another question. Mrs. Watts might become suspicious of the inquisitor unless he could convey to her that he was a disappointed friend, a close friend. "I did want to see Miss Dubetat. Was she all right? Quite well, and that sort of thing?"

"Happen I didn't say a word to her. She seemed a bit glum, you might say. Quiet like."

"Poor girl!" Peter's new cunning told him how to lead the woman on. "She's been having a worrying time. I've been anxious about her. Nerves play such tricks, you know. Make you frightened of your own shadow."

"Funny you should say that!" Mrs. Watts was sympathetic and confidential. "It's just what I thought about her. She seemed frightened in a glum sort of way. I must say Mr. Murrison was kindness itself, and that Mr. Alfie, too! Wouldn't let her out of his sight."

"Do you know where she was staying in Bosverran?"

"That I don't. I never saw her before last night."

He thanked Mrs. Watts and hurried away. He had a sense of urgency, but did not know why or where he was hurrying to. The police? They would stare at him unbelievingly, and he would not be able to blame them. In their shoes he would be incredulous himself. The only direct statement he could make was that he had reason to believe Henry Braddock had disappeared. The reason? Because Henry Braddock had not turned up at Pero's Hotel. Anything beyond that would involve him in the fantasies of the searched house, of the fat man and the dark girl. And nothing about them could be clear or real. It was all wild supposition, and the more he thought about it, the more unreal it seemed.

If it could be assumed that Braddock was the writer of the articles attacking Britt, then it might be supposed that the girl had gone to the house on behalf of Britt. From this argument came the further assumption that some evidence existed in support of the charges made in the *Sunday Gazette*, and Britt wanted to get hold of it. This did not necessarily impugn the good faith or sincerity of Britt. The evidence might be false, or he might, at some time, have committed an indiscretion or become innocently involved in something that he wanted suppressed in view of the libel action. It was certainly an indiscretion to permit illegal entry upon another man's house, but the girl, in the simpering, hero-struck devotion of her kind, had probably acted on her own responsibility.

So far, with all its ifs and buts, the theory was feasible, it was even reasonable. It was when you attempted to fit Mr. Murrison and Alfie into the pattern that the thing became confused, and the more Peter thought about it, the more was confusion confounded. Braddock had feared some enemy, but he had certainly not identified Murrison with that enemy; not, at any rate, before the evening of his departure.

And any charge Peter might make against Murrison – if he went to the police, that is – could be based only on the wildest suppositions. If he were rash enough to state that Murrison had taken the girl off to London against her will, the only reason he could give was that the girl had seemed frightened. The only witness he could quote was Mrs. Watts, and he was conscious that he had asked her leading questions. To hear what you want to hear, ask leading questions, especially when dealing with a woman like Mrs. Watts.

For all he knew, he, not Murrison, might have been the cause of the girl's fright. She had realised her mistake in saying his name and feared that he would cause trouble. Perhaps she had looked back and seen him following her. Perhaps Murrison and Alfie merely had been coming round the skytip in their battered car and she had welcomed them as rescuers. Perhaps they had told her of their imminent departure for London, and she had asked them to take her with them. Perhaps the big cream car with *Excalibur* on the door –

He checked himself. The perhapses were worse than the ifs and buts. They curbed his footsteps and weakened his resolution. They brought him to a standstill outside the post-office.

Wavering, he looked back in the direction of the police station. He could not now believe that there was a case for police intervention. Braddock would turn up, and nothing of any consequence would happen to the girl. It was nonsense to suppose that Murrison could have carted her off by force. If she had needed help, she would have called on Mrs. Watts. She could have made a fuss at her own lodging when she went for her suitcases. Or had she been too frightened to speak out?

He didn't know. In all the suppositions there was nothing he could hold to as a fact. One doubt, the authorship of the attacks on Britt, might have been resolved had he opened the letter from the *Sunday Gazette*, but it was too late for that now. He had dropped that letter through the slot of the posting-box before he learned that Braddock had failed to reach Pero's. If he had found out that J. Woodforde Bayles really was another of Braddock's pen-names, he would have established the motive for the girl's intervention. Now he could proceed only on guess-work. Unless....

There was a simple way to settle this one point, and the thought of it called him to action. He had gone on past the post office. He wheeled abruptly and went back. A few minutes later he was in the 'phone booth again, asking for Mr. Woodforde Bayles.

"You want the editorial department." The switchboard girl of the *Sunday Gazette* had a completely impersonal voice. "Just a moment."

She could not, of course, tell him that Woodforde Bayles did not exist. No one was likely to tell him that. He could learn the truth only by implication. He must mark each phrase and inflection, each hesitation, each evasion. He was tense, waiting for the next voice, though he was already sure that he had made his point. That non-committal phrase of the telephonist was enough. "You want the editorial department." If there were such a person as Bayles, she would have said: "He's in the editorial department. I'll put you through." Something like that.

A tired baritone sounded in his ear. An underling, no doubt. A messenger.

"Editorial department."

"I wish to speak to Mr. Bayles, Mr. Woodforde Bayles." Peter used an authoritative tone. It conveyed deliberately an affirmation of belief in Mr. Bayles with the object of provoking a definite reaction, an evasion that would leave him without doubt.

The reaction seemed evasive enough, but there was nothing in it to confirm conviction.

"I'll see if he's in, sir. Will you hold the line, please?"

Now, of course, would come someone in charge. He would be asked to state his business, but he had the answer to that one. He would say it was personal business and demand to speak to the supposed

Bayles himself. He could not ask straight out whether Bayles was, in fact, Braddock, because he knew such information would never be given to an unknown inquirer at the other end of a telephone line.

Waiting with the receiver clamped to his ear, he heard footsteps in London, firm steps on a tiled floor. A tap, a slight clatter.

"Bayles here," said a voice.

Peter swallowed hard.

"Bayles?" he said helplessly. "You mean you're really Woodforde Bayles?"

A laugh. "There's a suspicion round here to that effect. I've always shared it. Who's speaking? What can I do for you?"

The voice was light and pleasant, suggesting good humour and friendliness. Peter floundered in embarrassment. He hadn't planned to carry the thing this far. He didn't know what to say. This Woodforde Bayles might never have heard of Braddock. On the other hand –

He clutched at the straw. Apart from telling the man that he had merely telephoned to find out if he existed, there was nothing else he could do.

"I'm a friend of Henry Braddock's," he said, as if that might explain everything.

It did. The effect was startling. All the pleasantness and good humour went from the voice at the other end. It became sharp and sour and contemptuous.

"I've told Braddock what he can do." The words crackled. "I wrote to him yesterday. I don't intend to talk to an intermediary. You can tell him from me that he'd better make up his mind, and make it up quickly. That's all I've got to say to you, and don't call me up again."

Crash!

The indignant Mr. Bayles had hung up. All Mr. Ackland had got for his money was the suggestion that he was some kind of lackey.

Crash! Mr. Ackland's receiver replied belatedly to the insult. He was hot with anger before he got outside the post office. The rage in him mounted as he strode along the road to the farm.

To the devil with the lot of them. He was through with them, finished. Why should he give a damn about Braddock? Or the girl?

She could get herself abducted a dozen times, if there was anyone imbecile enough to abduct her. And the uncouth Bayles, that cheap reporter, that libellous muckraker – he was a fitting candidate for the group. That was enough! He would forget the lot of them.

Passing the Braddock house he looked involuntarily at the overflow pipe. It was more offensive than ever, but it wasn't leaking. As if he cared! The damned thing could drip till it flooded the countryside. He'd never go inside the place again. Never.

The rage was still on him when he sat down to the midday meal, but, by the time Mrs. Tregethney brought him plums and cream for dessert, he was beginning to think more calmly.

He stirred his coffee for a long time. He sat over it for a long time.

The kitchen tap dripped onto a cutting board in the sink.

Plack ... plack ... plack....

His coffee was cold. He pushed it aside, got up, and went to the kitchen door to speak to Mrs. Tregethney.

"I'm going up to town on the night train," he told her. "I want you to keep my room for me, please. I'll be back in a few days."

"I hope there's nothing wrong, Mr. Ackland?" Mrs. Tregethney gazed at him a little curiously.

"No, nothing's wrong." He tried to put lightness into it. "Just some unexpected business."

Chapter 8

THE offices of the National League of Patriots were not impressive. You went along Floral Street, turned to the left, marked the painted shingle above the tarnished brass plate of *Kitts and Botten Sons, Fruit Importers*, and ascended a narrow, much worn stairway to what might once have been the loft floor of a banana warehouse. The conversion into rooms and cubicles had been accomplished by the use of quite a lot of plaster-board and plywood, and the whole lay-out suggested the bleak utility of a polling booth at a by-election.

When he pushed open the door at the head of the stairs, Peter Ackland thought for a moment that he had blundered upon the premises of *Kitts and Botten Sons*, but a framed camera study of Arthur Lamorak-Britt reassured him. It was handsome, it was noble, a pledge of devotion to the chivalrous ideal; but it got no help from the antique round table in the middle of the boarded floor. The table was antique only in the sense that it had been made some time ago. It looked cheap and decrepit, but it had enough strength left to bear some pamphlets and printed leaflets and a sign in Old English that said: PLEASE TAKE ONE.

The reception cubicle was small. If Galahad, say, had sought an interview with the new leader, he would have had to leave his lance and shield downstairs. There was just room for the table, a couple of chairs, and a bell-button.

Peter pushed the bell-button. He heard the subdued snarl of a buzzer through a fluttering of typewriter keys and the whirring of typewriter carriages. Patriotism was evidently a brisk business, calling for a formidable amount of correspondence.

A panel in the plaster-board partition slid open to disclose a well-groomed blonde.

This, thought Peter without enthusiasm, was more like it. This broke the bleakness with a golden gleam.

She looked like something by Burne-Jones, except that she was alive. She might have been a resurrected Elaine reduced by modern conditions to earning her keep as a receptionist, the lily maid of Astolat on a pay-as-you-earn basis.

Experimenting with a French pronunciation, Peter asked for Miss Dubetat.

The blonde corrected him. "Miss Dubetat? Have you an appointment?"

"No. Just give her my name, please. Mr. Ackland."

"Will you take a seat for a moment?"

From the manner of the girl it was to be inferred that Miss Dubetat was definitely on the premises. Of course, he had never really believed in his fantasy of abduction. Nevertheless, he had a deep feeling of relief, so deep that he became alarmed. It was ridiculous, he told himself. Why should he have the least concern about the dark girl, especially after the way she had deceived him over the imaginary Forbes and his Bosveor Cottage? She was obviously the sort who would get herself into serious trouble sooner or later, but it had nothing to do with him. He could not go about acting as guardian to every stupid, self-willed, dishonest and reckless hussy he happened to encounter through no fault of his own. Who did she think he was, anyway? One of those moonstruck hobbledehoys of the Round Table? A *Gareth*, a *Galahad*, a *Geraint*? Why did so many of their silly names begin with G?

The blonde opened a plywood door and appeared full length in the rest of her natty business suit. She looked even better than she had through the hole in the partition.

"Miss Dubetat is very busy this morning," she announced. "Can I do anything for you, or would you prefer to make an appointment?"

"Neither, thanks. I'll wait." That was probably impolite, but he didn't care. He was determined to get an explanation of the invasion of Braddock's house. Braddock had not yet turned up at Pero's Hotel, and the dark girl might know something about his movements. Further, Peter wanted to know what was the link-up with Mr. Murrison and Alfie. A night on the train to Paddington had not quieted his suspicions. He was going to be ruthless. If necessary he would threaten to go to the police.

The blonde girl said: "I'm afraid it will be useless to wait."

"I'll risk it," Peter told her. "I've plenty of time. If Miss Dubetat doesn't want to talk to me, I'll have to see Mr. Britt."

"That's impossible. He's booked up for weeks. He has practically no time while the House is sitting." Her tone had become reverent. "We scarcely ever see him while the House is sitting" she added, with the suspicion of a sigh.

"Doesn't he come in here to get his letters, to attend to things, to run the office?"

"Indeed, no. Miss Dubetat runs the office. Mr. Britt sees his secretaries at the House, or at his flat. He's so busy, he has to have three secretaries to take his letters." Enthusiasm for the great man made her garrulous, and Peter saw that she could not help but talk about him to anyone who would listen. Also, he saw that she was no more than a child, and he felt sorry for her. When you get to be thirty-five you begin to appreciate the pathos of youth, the pathos of credulity, the pathos of all the little self-deceptions, illusions, pretences. She was at that teen age when she must make every effort to appear the woman of poise, of mature judgment, and almost every movement, every inflection, betrayed her.

Peter said: "I suppose Miss Dubetat is one of the three secretaries?"

"Not at all." There was scorn in her voice, whether for his ignorance or for Miss Dubetat, he couldn't decide. "She never leaves the office," the child added.

"Except when she goes to Cornwall."

"Cornwall?" The wide blue eyes were puzzled.

"You'd better tell her that I'm staying till she sees me," he suggested.

"Is it about the Youth Clubs?"

"No. It's about the Forbes property, Bosveor Cottage. Just tell her that. She'll understand."

"I'll try."

It worked, or something did. The girl returned in a moment and held the door open. She smiled. "Will you come this way?"

Beyond the door was the stenographic department, but the keys of the machines were at rest. The typists had paused for elevenses, and cups and saucers stood on shorthand notebooks. There were six or seven of the girls and their skill as operators must have been incidental, for surely they had been chosen as potential material for a glamour chorus? Perhaps Mr. Britt had some plans for an Arthurian pageant or ballet? Put these willowy creatures in pre-Raphaelite robes and set them down in a magic garden to play ball, and you'd need nothing more than music by Stravinsky. They were all here for the casting director — Enid, Lynnette Iseult, Ettarre.

"This way, Mr. Ackland."

He pulled himself together.

Elaine opened a door in another plaster-board partition and motioned him in. There was a flat-topped desk in a small room, a desk of such dimensions that it seemed to occupy nearly all the available space. There was, however, other furniture; a couple of small chairs, a filing-cabinet, a bookcase, and a very large painting in oils of Arthur Lamorak-Britt. Seated at the desk beneath the painting was a diminutive woman with frizzy grey hair and rimless pince-nez. She was correcting a galley-proof, and continued to read with intense concentration as he entered.

Peter looked inquiringly at his guide, but she was looking at the middle button of the portrait's waistcoat.

He felt a little irritated — and puzzled. If this were an ante-room, it didn't seem to lead anywhere. Outside the window, behind the frizzy-haired woman, there was watery sunshine. Noises penetrated — the hoot of motor-horns and the other sounds of Covent Garden market. Peter listened. In a lull of immediate activity, he could hear the distant purr of traffic in the Strand.

He drew a deep, impatient breath. He was about to speak when the woman at the desk put down her pen and raised her head. She had pale small eyes in an intense, elderly face. He thought she looked like a governess in a play by Tchekov. She took off her pince-nez and held them in an attitude that suggested a hiker about to hitch a ride. Then she smiled archly.

"Well, well, well!" she said. "So this is the young man who couldn't take no for an answer. Sit down, young man. I can see you're good timber, the very sort we want in our movement. Enthusiasm, energy, stick-to-itiveness. In short, good timber." The smile sweetened horribly. "You'd make an excellent organiser for one of our youth clubs. You know: bringing up the young idea to a sense of civic responsibility. In each rising generation there is a terrific dynamic force to be canalised, don't you think?"

"I haven't thought much about it. I – "

"Yes, yes. It is so." The pince-nez swivelled to point, at him. "A little indoctrination at the right time, and the battle's won. It is demonstrable. Give youth faith, a belief in the cause, and youth will move mountains." Without waiting for any comment, she turned to the indoctrinated blonde, who was still gazing at the great icon. "That will do, Millie. You can send this proof back to the printer."

Millie jumped, reached for the proof, and withdrew.

"Now, young man." The pince-nez described some angular pattern in the air. "What's all this about a man named Forbes and some cottage? I don't understand."

He had been pushing back the thought that this was Miss Dubetat in front of him, but now it could not be evaded. She was, all too plainly, the Aunt Primrose of the *Gazette* article. Twice within twenty-four hours he had had to face up to a false conclusion, but this time he was not embarrassed by the sense of anticlimax. Error had served him by bringing him so far. Now he must make the most of the advantage gained; conceal his mistake and require the woman to send for the dark girl.

"I thought you would know about Forbes and Bosveor Cottage," he said. "If you don't, I'd better talk to the girl who saw me in Cornwall two days ago."

"Splendid. You must do that," said Miss Dubetat, "though," she went on briskly, "I don't see what it has to do with me. Are you suggesting that this girl is one of my staff?"

"She made it clear that she was one of Mr. Britt's staff."

"Impossible." The pince-nez jerked accusingly in his direction. "No one has been in Cornwall. Our chief has been too occupied with affairs in his own constituency."

"I'm sorry, but I must insist. Negotiations were entered into. The girl was in Bosverran two days and for some days before that. A tall, dark girl, with dark eyes. She might even be described as beautiful."

"I, also, must insist. I am in full control of all the female staff. Someone seems to have made quite an impression on you. Why she should represent herself as a member of our organisation, I can't make out. She might, of course, belong to the N.L.P. That, no doubt, is the explanation."

"Let me ask you a question." Peter leaned across the desk and picked up a printer's proof of *Excalibur* held above the waters. "This is the symbol of your League, isn't it?"

"Quite so."

"And you have it painted on the doors of the cars you use?"

"Certainly."

"Well, then, I saw this girl riding in one of your cars in Bosverran High Street a few days ago. A large cream-coloured car, chauffeur-driven."

"You're beginning to alarm me, Mr. Ackland." The pince-nez were placed back on her nose. "It's a fact that Mr. Britt keeps such a car at his house near Camelford, but no one has authority to use it, and no one in authority has visited the property in some months."

He was being brushed off. Or was she telling the truth? He couldn't accuse her of lying when he wasn't sure. He might suspect it, but what real basis was there for suspicion? You could so easily deceive yourself when you felt a sudden and instinctive aversion to someone. She was so like that Tchekov governess, he expected her to produce a pack of cards and ask him to pick one out. In effect he felt that this was what she had already done. Underneath that frizzy-haired spinsterish silliness, she was clever. She was too clever for him, and this made him dislike her the more.

"You alarm me considerably, young man," she repeated. "So far as I am aware, the car was locked up in the garage. Until now, we've found the caretaker quite trustworthy. I must get in touch with him at once. If necessary, we shall invoke the police. Where did you say you saw the car? Boskerran?"

Put the card back in the pack and shuffle. Shuffle well.

"Bosverran," he said distinctly. "You can't make me believe that you don't know Bosverran?"

"Make you believe, young man!" She took off the pince-nez and stared at him. "Why should I make you believe anything? Is there any particular reason why I should know Bosverran?"

"Yes, there is." He gave her stare for stare. "Henry Braddock lives there."

"A local celebrity?" She smirked, and he could have thrown her ormolu inkstand at her. "I'm afraid I never heard of him. Young man, I'm sure you are genuinely disturbed about something, but why come to me? Not that I have no wish to help you –" she looked at her wristwatch – "on the contrary, but I am a very busy person. Now, what did this girl do to you, and why are you so sure she's an employee of the organisation? Anyone may go joy-riding in a borrowed car."

"I saw her at one of your meetings in Kensington. She was acting as a steward, as one in authority."

On went the pince-nez. "My dear young man, every local meeting has its proportion of young things as stewards! Most of them adore our leader. You can't blame them for that, but it does dispose them to assert themselves. Rather charming in a way. I can't find it in my heart to discourage them. The fear I have is that you may have encountered an extreme case. An emotionally unbalanced person might make claims contrary to fact, might even bribe a servant to take her riding in the adored one's car. We have had our unfortunate incidents. I hope you've not been victimised in any way."

The queen of spades again! Beware of a dark woman.

"I've not been victimised," he said. "Not yet."

"Then what brings you here? What business have you with this girl? What exactly is your trouble?"

The last question pulled him up with a jolt. He had no answer for it except that he was a fool. One thing was clear. He could get nothing out of this frizzy-haired governess. If she was not genuinely ignorant, she was quite determined to pretend that she was, and he knew he could not break her down. To answer her, to keep a semblance of reason in the thing, he followed the dark girl's example and made up a tale about a cottage. The girl had been looking for a cottage, and he had found one for her. He had promised to notify her, he added lamely.

The pince-nez came off again and she stared at him.

"You came all the way to London to tell a complete stranger about a cottage?"

"No. I happened to be here. My business is in London."

"What is your business, Mr. Ackland?"

"Quite unimportant." He got to his feet. "I'm sorry I've taken up your valuable time."

She pushed a button on her desk.

"Not at all," she said. "I'm grateful for your warning about the car. I'll go into the matter at once."

The blonde came to pilot him through the outer office. She smiled. She was quite friendly now. He had been received; he had won his spurs. You had to get somewhere before you were anybody in Astolat. She had an effective smile, ingenuous. The effect was of complete innocence. He wondered how stupid she really was. He wondered, also, if he could put over an unrehearsed line. He had no opinion of himself as an actor, but there was everything to gain, certainly nothing to lose. He waited till they came to the outer door, till they were shut off from the others in the little reception-room with the pamphlets on the round table and the sign that said: PLEASE TAKE ONE.

"Confound it!" he exclaimed. "I should have made a note. I can never remember names. Who was the girl who made the trip to Cornwall? Miss Dubetat did tell me."

"That would be Jessica – "

The answer had come automatically, but was halted abruptly. The beautiful blue eyes gazed at him quite without expression, but the ingenuous smile flickered and went out.

"When do you mean?" she asked.

"Last week. What's Jessica's surname?"

"No." The blonde shook her head. "She was out there in the spring. At St. Ives. For a whole fortnight. I don't know if anyone was in Cornwall last week." The smile came back. "Shall I ask Miss Dubetat for you?"

He said: "It doesn't matter all that much. Who's this Jessica?"

"Just a girl who used to work here. She left." The blonde looked round, then lowered her voice. "She couldn't get on with Aunt Primrose." The smile was full of innocent fun. "They had a real set-to."

"She wouldn't have been a tall, dark girl, by any chance?"

"Who? Jessica? Goodness, no! She was ginger."

The blonde gave him a final, farewell smile and delivered him to the dark, narrow staircase. He still wondered how stupid she really was, and continued to wonder as he walked away over the market cobbles.

Because he had taken a dislike to Miss Dubetat, it did not follow that she had been trying to fob him off with a false story. Because he believed that the blonde girl was slow-witted, it was not to be assumed that he had trapped her into a vital admission. If he had, she had been sharp enough to recover, so one way or another he was up against a contradiction.

The trouble was that each leap he had made at a conclusion had carried him into a fresh bog of uncertainty. He must make no more of these wild leaps. They were the mistakes of the amateur. The trained investigator would never commit them. The trained investigator would observe, examine, analyse, follow up, never deviating from a logical line of thought and action. Peter found himself in Long Acre. He turned into Drury Lane and walked down towards the Aldwych, trying to put the better principles into practice as he did so.

This story of the stolen or borrowed car was absurd, though not impossible. It was absurd to him because he could see no feasible motive. Granted that this dark girl had wanted to create an impression that she had official connection with the National League of Patriots, would she have gone to all the trouble to get the car from a locked garage miles away in the Camelford district. Merely to display the symbol of *Excalibur* in Bosverran? And for whose benefit? Anyway she was connected with the N.L.P. He had first-hand knowledge of that, for she had certainly been active in some official capacity at that meeting in Kensington, Of course, like the ginger Jessica of the blonde girl's story, she might have had a real set-to with Aunt Primrose and been told to go. She had become the enemy of the N.L.P. She had plotted some scheme of revenge. Because of her knowledge it had been easy enough to use the car, but, again, why borrow a car in Camelford merely to go to Bosverran? And why Bosverran?

The answer was Braddock.

Peter followed the curve of the Aldwych to the Strand and went on along Fleet Street.

The whole business was linked up with the articles in and the threat of a libel suit against the *Sunday Gazette*.

And Braddock was the link. Braddock had something that they were after, all of them: the *Gazette* reporter, the dark girl, the fat man. A little storm had gathered about Braddock in the clay country, and Braddock had fled. He had deliberately disappeared, and he would turn up only in his own good time.

"Where's Patterfield Court? Somewhere round here, isn't it?"

The messenger-boy directed him. At the *Gazette* office he asked for Woodforde Bayles. He gave his card to a commissionaire; his business card with the name of the firm in the corner; Frayne and Copley, Architects. Bayles didn't know him by name, anyway.

He was thinking: Bayles knows why Braddock is the link. He must tell me. He'll surely see the responsibility that I have. He's had contact with Braddock. He must explain. Now.

The commissionaire came back from a house 'phone behind the lift-shaft.

"Mr. Bayles isn't in at present sir. Is there any message?"

"Do you know when he'll be in?"

"I don't sir. Except that he usually looks in around six."

"Thank you."

Fleet Street was unfamiliar territory. He found a restaurant and had something to eat. His nerves were beginning to tighten; the clatter of plates was awful. Outside again, the traffic began to bother him. It was worse than before he went to Cornwall.

He returned to the *Gazette,* and the commissionaire, after another telephone inquiry, shook his head.

"I'd try around six, if I were you, sir," he said. "That's the safest time. If Mr. Bayles comes in, I'll tell him. I've sent up your card."

He went along Farringdon Street, climbed to Holborn Viaduct, and continued towards Bloomsbury. The earlier sunshine had gone, and the sky was darkened by a fog that looked as if it might later come down to ground level.

Gladdon Street. Pero's Hotel again. The cramped entrance hall, where everything seemed to be on top of you, was gloomier, shabbier than it had seemed that morning, when he had first called there. Inside, the fog gave a brownish tint to the opaline bowls of the ceiling lights. He squeezed past a wardrobe trunk and the automatic lift and reached the reception desk. There was a new clerk on duty, so he would have to start from the beginning.

"Could you tell me, please, if a Mr. Henry Braddock has arrived?"

The clerk's hand flicked the pages of a formidable book. "Braddock. Name seems familiar, but he's not registered. Just a minute." Out came the letters from the pigeon-hole marked A-B. "I thought so. There's mail waiting for him, but no, sir, he hasn't arrived yet."

Word for word, gesture for gesture, the scene of the morning was repeated, but now it had a more depressing effect on Peter. He saw the letters he had re-addressed from Cornwall, including the one with the imprint of the *Sunday Gazette* on the envelope. If he could read that letter, he might know what it was that Bayles wanted from Henry Braddock; what they all wanted from Braddock. There it was, not two feet away from him on the age-darkened mahogany of the counter. He could reach out a hand and touch it.

"No, sir. No sign of him yet. No reservation, either. Hold on a bit! Cornwall? I remember now. He stayed with us last year. He should be here pretty soon if his mail is being sent on. Maybe he's on the day train. Gets in at Paddington round five. Why don't you try at half-past five or so?"

The clerk gathered the letters together, held them with one hand, smacked them against the palm of the other, then pushed them back in the pigeon-hole.

If he tried about half-past five and there was another clerk on duty, he could claim that he was Henry Braddock and ask for the letters. Then he could find out what Bayles had written.

Impossible. It was not to be done.

If he were asked to show his identity card, what then? If the clerk remembered Henry Braddock? He would be exposed in a serious offence. The police would come. . . .

The police? If Bayles should be obstinate, he would go to the police. He would establish that Henry Braddock had disappeared, that his house had been ransacked. He would suggest that Braddock was being held out of sight somewhere, that he had been kidnapped. The police would have power to open the letter, all the letters.

Half-past five? He shook his head. He knew that Braddock was not on the train, and it would be useless to come back. He thanked the clerk and turned away. Outside on the pavement he felt very tired. He had had little sleep on the train last night. After breakfast at Paddington and a brief visit to his flat in South Kensington for a wash and a clean shirt, he had begun his round: Pero's, Britt's office, Fleet Street, Pero's again. He was trembling, he was so tired. There was a weight dragging at his shoulders, pulling him down.

He wavered in the middle of the pavement. A taxi discharged a fare, and he got in the cab, giving his South Kensington address. He remembered lights from offices shining through the yellowing air of Shaftesbury Avenue. There was a halt at Piccadilly Circus. Then he must have dozed because the next thing, the cab-driver had pushed back the glass panel and was talking to him.

"You're there, sir."

He paid the man and went up the steps to the front door. The drowsiness on him would not be shaken off. He fumbled with his key before he got the door open. Inside the hall he behaved automatically, switching on the light, looking to see if there was any mail in the letter-box. A couple of letters for Dixon and one for May, the other tenants of the small converted house. He listened for a moment, but there was no sound. The charwoman would have finished up hours ago, and Dixon and May would be at their jobs till evening. He left the letters on the hall table and climbed the two flights of stairs to his top flat. The bulbs on the time switch snapped off as he reached his door. It was almost like night on the landing, but inside the flat the windows admitted a fog-filtered twilight.

There was relief in the thought of being home, in the knowledge that he could relax, in the feeling of familiar things, of order and peace. Because he was sure that everything must be as it always had been, he was not very observant at once. Or the drowsiness was too much for him. He closed his eyes in the first moment. He stood in the narrow hall in a half-stupor, and it was a delightful thought that he need no longer fight against his weariness. He'd have a drink. Then he'd set the alarm and sleep.

It was when he opened the door of his living-room to get his drink that he was shocked into wakefulness. He felt, in the first instant, that this was like going back to the house that Braddock had left. Then he felt a more personal impact, and he was rigid, on the threshold, in dismay. These were his things that were strewn about and overturned and left awry. When he moved from startled contemplation of the disorder, he saw that a box at the end of the hall had also come in for attention. He went to the bedroom, then to the bathroom and the kitchenette. Everywhere it was the same, everywhere papers had been thrown down after a hasty examination, the contents of drawers tipped out and scattered, books taken from their shelves and dropped on the floor.

When he had seen the whole of the flat, he had no feeling but of fury. He went to the 'phone and started to dial. Nine . . . The wheel swung slowly back. Nine . . . The wheel was too slow. He had time to think. He put the receiver back and sat at his ransacked desk. He closed his eyes, and his head nodded in weariness again as he became calmer, trying to reason and plan. He must not call the police till he knew what he was doing. There was the girl . . . He must take no step he might regret. Wait. See Woodforde Bayles. Demand explanations.

Another wave of anger started in him, but fell away. Reaction drained the last of his energy. He closed his eyes, and it took him quite an effort to get them open again. He picked up the alarm clock and went into the bedroom.

Chapter 9

THE commissionaire at the *Gazette* offices was right.

Bayles came in a few minutes after six, and Peter got up from his chair when the man in uniform gave him a sign. Bayles was a smiling, frank-looking man who might have been anything between thirty and forty. He was quite easy and friendly till the name of Braddock was mentioned. Then the smile left his face and he froze. He stared at Peter.

He said: "I suppose you're the bird who telephoned? How do you come into the business? Can't Braddock do his own dirty work?"

Peter tried to keep calm. "I don't know what you're talking about. I'm not mixed up in any dirty work. I want to know what's become of Braddock?"

"Save it!" said Bayles contemptuously. "I told you I don't like intermediaries. However, now that you're here, you'd better come upstairs."

"Now wait a minute! I want – "

Bayles cut in on him. "You needn't be afraid. I haven't got the C.I.D. in my filing cabinet. Not even a dictaphone. Only don't let's have any misunderstandings. By rights, I ought to get a Scotland Yard man along and have him talk to you."

"Perhaps you'd better do that," Peter snapped. "You're too busy jumping to conclusions to listen yourself. Didn't you hear what I said? I want to know where Braddock is. If you can't or won't help me, then I'm going to Scotland Yard myself. Braddock's mixed up with you in some way over this League of Patriots business, and I want to know how. Maybe you won't talk to me, but you'll have to talk to Scotland

Yard."

Bayles stared again, then motioned towards the lift. Three floors up he took Peter into a small room.

"All right. Let's have it," he said. "What do you want?"

Peter let him have it. He was brief, but covered the essential points. He spoke rapidly to forestall interruptions.

"Well?" he demanded at last, "what's it all about? Braddock was in touch with you. He came to town to see you. Where is he?"

Bayles thought for a moment. His manner had changed during Peter's recital. He pursed his lips.

"How do you know he came to town to see me?"

"I don't know. I've a feeling."

"You may be right, but I haven't seen him. More likely he came to see Britt."

"Then why hasn't he turned up at Pero's? Who is this fat man, this Murrison? Do you know him?"

"Nordic Nat." Bayles grinned. "He's another of the old guard Hitler-worshippers. When Britt discovered patriotism, Murrison was in the first rush for the penitent's bench. He believes in making politics pay. That's his plank on any platform. I've rather wondered why Britt took him into the fold. Probably had no choice. When you've had his sort of past, things keep on bobbing up. I don't know about this little fellow, this Alfie. He's a new one on me."

"There was a girl in it. Perhaps you know about her?"

Peter had been keeping her out of it, afraid to mention her. He didn't trust Bayles. If the reporter could use the girl in his attacks upon Britt, he would treat her as mercilessly as he had treated Primrose Dubetat. He would be on the scent of any scandal or anything that might look like scandal, with the quickness of a ferret. But Peter had to find out somehow about the girl, and he saw that he could not keep her out of the business altogether for the simple reason that quite obviously she was deeply in it. If Murrison was one of Britt's agents and she another, it was not feasible that they could have been in Bosverran on different missions. There could be only one alternative to the suggestion of collusion. She might be the girl called Jessica who had quarrelled with Miss Dubetat. She might have been in Bosverran to counter a move by Murrison. She might have been acting for this man Woodforde Bayles. The description of Jessica as ginger could have been a belated attempt by the receptionist at the League office to cover up.

"What girl?" Bayles said quickly.

"A dark girl," Peter said. "Rather good-looking. Tall and – well, tall and dark. It's just possible her name could be Jessica."

Bayles sighed wearily. "Jessica Trask!" A frown showed troubled concern, or annoyance, or both. "I told the little fool to keep out of it. How did you run across her?"

Peter furnished more details.

"Little fool!" Bayles repeated savagely. "I warned her. Feloniously entering a person's house! Jeepers! Heaven knows what she'll be doing next for that inflated toad."

"You mean Britt?"

"Who else?"

"She still works for him?"

"Unfortunately."

So the blonde at the office had invented the quarrel story to retrieve her bad error in blurting out the name. It might seem a little silly, but, come to think of it, so did Miss Dubetat's suggestion about the car's being taken from the Camelford house without authority. It was obvious now that Britt had sent Jessica Trask down to Bosverran in that car, probably to instruct Murrison. Or to watch him? To make sure?

To make sure of what?

Fear loomed at that moment, and, strangely, it was not for Braddock. It was the girl he saw now as the prospective victim of the plot.

"What's happened to Braddock?" he demanded sharply.

"What could happen?" Bayles snapped out the answer as if the question had put him on edge. "It's pretty obvious he went off somewhere with Murrison and this other fellow. No doubt they played a trick on him to get him out of the way so that they could search his house. Probably they persuaded him to go over to this

Camelford place of Britt's. Most likely he'd been angling to see Britt, and who knows, Britt may have been at Camelford that night."

"Braddock was afraid for his life. He carried a pistol or something. I tell you he was a scared man."

"That sort of chap always is. It gets to be a habit with them. Did he tell you how he used to run round Europe before the war?"

"Yes. He mentioned his books."

"The student of politics, eh? Good cover for any bit of business that came his way. He didn't mention, I suppose, that he was once picked up in Prague as a spy? That was the time of the Sudeten experiment. The police broke up a ring of Nazi operators. Years ago, but it's the same old Braddock."

"You mean Braddock was in Hitler's pay?"

"I mean he was floating with the scum. The police had no evidence against him, so they slammed him across the frontier. My own opinion is he was in no one's pay. He just couldn't keep his nose clean. Do you know his book *A Study in Terrorism*? That gives you the picture. He could always put up the tale that he was collecting material, but if the material brought him some cash on the side, why not? The whole thing reeks of back-alley cafes and bead curtains. I've no doubt he was ready to pick up a penny wherever he saw it. He'd be chasing the illusion that there's big money in it, and there never is. There are only pennies and a seedy bunch of petty crooks with their hands out."

Peter saw Braddock waiting in one of those grim alleys, teetering, pigeon-toed. He saw him hurrying anxiously along a dark street of foreign houses, looking back over his shoulder.

Bayles said: "Murrison's another typical specimen, a man after Braddock's own heart. I've no doubt they get on well together."

"I don't know." Peter's doubts would not be allayed. "Braddock was really scared. I'm sure of it."

"I tell you it's a habit with birds like Braddock. He wouldn't have much to fear from Murrison, anyway. That fat fake wouldn't risk his little finger, let alone his neck. And what chance can Britt take? One slip and he's out on his ear with his crackpot empire on top of him."

But Peter had the uncomfortable feeling that Bayles was trying to reassure himself.

"Even if Braddock went willingly with Murrison," he argued, "they must be holding him against his will. That's pretty serious in itself."

"How are you going to bring a charge when you're trying to work a spot of blackmail?" Bayles asked.

"So that's what it is?"

"That's what it is." The newspaper man was positive in his words yet the worrying uncertainty persisted in his voice. "Braddock found something while he was with Amgot in Germany. He claims it will prove my case against Britt. When I started the articles, he wrote me that he had some good material but he wasn't giving it away. I told him I didn't buy pigs in pokes, but he kept at me. He gave me a few hints about Britt. Probably he had a hunch there'd have to be a libel suit. Nothing could serve him better in his game of playing one side against the other. Did he give you any explanation of this London trip?"

"He said he expected to collect some money that was owing to him."

"He expected to collect some money, period. The time had come to sell to the highest bidder."

"What is it he has to sell?"

"He wouldn't say. Too cagey. A letter, a document, a photograph? Who knows? Apparently the search of the house failed, or Braddock would have been turned loose. Braddock could be pretty stubborn if he wanted to. They might try a little ill-treatment on him, a bread-and-water diet, solitary confinement. Of course, they may have got what they want by now. We don't know what's been going on the last couple of days. Braddock could have taken a price and gone back to his house."

"Not up to to-day," Peter asserted.

Bayles shrugged. He seemed to have convinced himself at last. "What makes you so sure?" he asked.

"Some time before three this afternoon my flat was entered and searched. It was all right when I left it about ten this morning."

Bayles jerked himself up in his chair. He stared at Peter for quite a few seconds.

"Your flat!" he said. "You! This is getting interesting." He rose slowly and reached for his hat. "It's time, I think, we paid a visit to a friend of mine. Do you mind?"

Peter followed him back to the lift.

"Where are we going?" he inquired.

"Not far," Bayles answered. "Just to have a word with Miss Jessica Trask. That's if she's home."

They found a taxi.

It seemed that Bayles had known the girl for years. His family and hers had been near neighbours. She had had a brother, and, in the days before the war, they had all been friends – Bayles, Benny Trask, and kid sister. She had worshipped her big brother, and, when he left for the war, he was the greatest hero in uniform. Bayles joined the Navy and lost touch. It was only when he returned from service in the Pacific that he heard of Benny's death as a prisoner-of-war in Germany. Then, back from Germany, had come Britt, bearing a letter from the dead brother, a letter miraculously preserved through all the dangers and hardships Britt had endured while, supposedly, on the run.

Britt, it seemed, had befriended Benny, had nursed him in illness, had somehow procured comforts for him. The letter was a curiously emotional tribute to the older man for his devotion, and it had its inevitable effect on Jessica. The hero was already sanctified, the halo sufficiently strong to throw an effulgence on the handsome countenance of Arthur Lamorak-Britt. She was, of course, at the romantic age. She resolved to repay devotion with devotion.

Bayles spoke bitterly. There was hatred of Britt in every mention of the name. Peter wondered how much of it sprang from jealousy. He didn't much like these revelations. Though he listened eagerly to every word, the sudden appearance of the man in the reporter was disconcerting. It was simply, he told himself, that he was embarrassed by this curious readiness of a stranger to make a confessional of the taxi that was taking them on a journey; but he was also aware of a discomfort that went deeper than embarrassment. It was mixed up with something he had been trying to evade ever since he saw Jessica Trask outside the post office in Bosverran. Or perhaps it went farther back, to the night of that meeting of the National League of Patriots.

"When Britt set up as a patriot," Bayles was saying, "she was at his side to take his notes and type his letters. She went through the election campaign with him, and she was as good as a dozen secretaries. I warned her about his past, but she wouldn't listen. She said people could learn from their mistakes and there were lots of people who had learned things from the war. She was sold on his brand of dope. She believed in him utterly. That was when I began to dig deeper into his recent past. I wanted to save her, but nothing I found had any effect. She just went on sitting at his muddy feet, for all the world as if she were madly in love with him."

"Wasn't she?" Peter hesitated over the question. The business was becoming altogether too painful.

"That's the queer thing about it. She never was. Not in plain down-to-earth terms. I don't think she ever saw Britt as a man. I know there are plenty of women swoon over him, but that's the bad taste some women have. Or maybe there are some things they don't mind. I mean when you know Britt, you know there's something not normal in his make-up. Something wanting. I don't think Jess has ever been aware of it. You've got to remember that she believes in him fully. He's a sort of demigod. His curly head is out of reach, up among the stars. Heaven knows what sort of emotional mechanism is involved, but it's all mixed up with that old worship of the hero-brother. You see how it is? She's a prisoner. There's no life for her while she's tied to this greasy monster. She calls it a career, and in a way I suppose it is. She's successful. He treats her well. He's looked after her from the time the racket began to pay dividends. He has his set of loyalties, I suppose. He pays her well. He's more than made up for the time she worked for nothing. But she's a prisoner all the same. She isn't living."

"Is this why you're trying to smash Britt?" The question came in a moment of suspense between a red and a green traffic light. It was inevitable, posing an issue not to be side-stepped.

Bayles seemed not to have heard.

"You know, Ackland, I've often wondered why the fellow ever delivered that letter from Benny Trask. It's very queer how a man who has no thought for anything outside himself and his own glorification will suddenly make a useless, sentimental gesture that may lead to his finish. You would say that any man in his senses would have torn up that letter while he was still with the Germans in Germany. Britt was in his senses all right, yet he carries out his mission. I hate the man's guts, but there's something almost human in that one spot of useless defiance."

"I don't follow you," Peter complained. "Why shouldn't he have delivered the letter?"

"The danger of it. Whatever he did in Germany, he covered up his tracks pretty thoroughly. After he was removed from the prisoners' camp to be taken to hospital, there's no evidence of contact with any other prisoner except this letter, and he brings that back to England himself. You see, Ackland, he might be confident enough that his own movements couldn't be traced, but he couldn't be sure about another man's movements, could he?"

Peter felt a little indignant. "You seem to base everything on your assumption that Britt was a traitor. I've read your articles. I can't say I'm convinced. From what you tell me about Braddock, his evidence may be a fake. The fact that Britt brings this letter to England could be proof that he's genuine. You might argue that."

"You might." The reporter's admission had all the condescension of a man with an ace up his sleeve. "I tried every way to get a line on Britt in Germany. I couldn't. But I ran across a man who had been in a camp with Benny Trask a year before he died. Do you know what this man told me? He told me the little rat sold out to the Nazis. He told me he could round up a dozen ex-prisoners to swear to it. Some of the other rats worked on Benny, softening him up, and he went away with them. There were good times to be had if you were willing to collaborate. Wine, woman, song – all the doings. Benny went outside the wire. When he died he was still outside the wire, and so was his friend Britt."

"I haven't seen anything of this in your articles."

"It's something I can't use, Ackland. I'd rather throw up the job than hurt Jess in that way. Anyway, I don't believe Benny was the complete rat, not fundamentally. He was just a small boy. He was the sort they'd pick out to work on. He liked a good time and he had no particular convictions. You could pull him any way you wanted. He'd do some damn fool thing one day, and cut off his hand to make up for it the next. When you call a man a rat, you have to be careful you're not flattering yourself."

Peter stared at him and saw a mask of malevolent concentration. It might have been a trick of light, of the faint, fog-dimmed glow of another traffic signal. He was becoming uncertain about this man, his inconsistencies. There was one measuring rod for Benny Trask; a different one for Britt. One had to be very careful of self-flattery.

Perhaps Bayles picked up some telepathic impulse. He said: "Don't make any error. Britt's a horse of another colour. I know about him. I'm certain. No doubt he was kind to Benny. A man's not wholly bad all the time, even when he's that kind of rat."

It was getting a bit mixed, zoologically. And Bayles was becoming sententious. For all the certainty he might proclaim, there seemed to be some anxiety in him. He was nervous and quick in speech, and his words bad a flavour of self-justification.

"Don't make any error," he repeated. "There's a world of difference between a deliberate policy and an act of impulse."

He paused as if to give Peter time to absorb this weighty statement, but his pauses were never long.

"You know, Ackland, Benny couldn't have realised what he was doing. He may have been a sick man, or half crazy. Once you're outside the wire, you're finished. There's no going back. There are only orders and threats. If you obey, you're all right. If you refuse, there's Belsen or Buchenwald. Unless there's a man like Britt to help you, for God knows what reason."

His contempt for Britt sharpened every word of the last sentence. Peter had a question to put, but Bayles went on.

"There's no evidence that Benny ever did anything for the enemy. Britt says they met in a prisoners' hospital, that Benny died of a wound received in an air-raid. There's no evidence of that, either, except Britt's word."

It seemed to Peter that there was no evidence of any sort. Through the cab window he saw the lights of houses dimmed down by the fog. Again he started to frame his question, but now the taxi spun in towards the kerb and pulled up, and Bayles sprang out and paid the driver. Bayles was quick in movement, quick and nervous as he was in speech. He crossed the pavement and mounted the steps to the front door of a small, narrow house. Peter stopped him as he was about to ring one of two bells.

"Wait a minute," he said. "I want to know about your articles in the *Gazette*. Did you suggest the attack on Britt, or was it the paper's idea?"

"I don't see that that need concern you." Bayles resented the question, or the interruption. "You think, I suppose, that I'm so worked up against the fellow I'd use the paper to exploit a personal grudge? You're wrong. I didn't suggest anything. I bucked against running the campaign. I told 'em to put anyone on it but leave me out. They insisted, mainly because I'd covered some of Britt's meetings. Now I'm on the job, I'm going to see it through. Do you mind?"

Nothing ran straight. Every time you sought for motives you came up against some twist, some inconsistency. Braddock was now portrayed as a crook, a blackmailer, Britt as a traitorous racketeer, Murrison as an unscrupulous hireling, the girl as a credulous romantic. What next? Braddock as the only innocent?

Bayles turned from the bell-push.

"This is going to be painful," he said. "If you have to pick me up in pieces, the office will inform my next-of-kin."

Perhaps it was merely an expression of nervous anxiety, but Peter did not like the quip. He was beginning to view Mr. Woodforde Bayles with some distaste.

And then the door opened.

Chapter 10

WHAT happened next was disconcerting to the already disconcerted Mr. Ackland.

The girl tried to slam the door in the reporter's face, but he had already got his foot across the threshold.

"Don't be in a hurry, Jess," he said. "We'd like to have a word with you."

"I've nothing to say to you," she answered him in a hard voice. "I told you that last time. I don't want to see you."

"I know, Jess, but we can't always have things the way we want them. Aren't you going to ask us in?"

"Will you go away?" Her voice rose in pitch and she made another vain effort to close the door.

"Now, now, you mustn't be discourteous!" Bayles spoke as a social worker to a delinquent child, gently, half-humorously, tolerantly, but with great firmness. "Mr. Ackland has come all the way from Cornwall to see you."

"Mr. Ackland!"

Her echo came in a sharp ejaculation. She must have seen the pair of them, but till now she had identified only Bayles. She peered past him, and he moved aside so that more light from the hall seeped out into the thin fog to reveal Peter. She was startled or puzzled. Startled was probably the word, and Bayles sought to improve the advantage gained.

"You seem to have bungled things at Bosverran," he said dryly. "Frankly, Jess, this role of political adventuress doesn't altogether suit you." The social worker allowed a note of mild reproof to creep in. "Breaking into other people's houses, and that sort of thing! Mr. Ackland is very upset. He has been threatening to go to Scotland Yard. But I persuaded him to come here first."

"You're close enough to Scotland Yard. You'd better go there." Her voice had a tremor in it. She spoke swiftly and fiercely as if she had a need to get the words out while she could.

Rage welled up in Bayles. The social worker vanished. "Listen," he said violently. "Even if you don't want to save yourself from scandal, you'd better think about your flounder-bellied friend Britt. I've talked to Ackland. If I had a sense of responsibility, he'd be with the police at this moment. Now, do you want a riot in the doorway, or do we go upstairs?"

She stepped back, and held the door open so that they could enter, then went ahead of them. Bayles slammed the door behind them. Her flat was one flight up, a conversion job of a type very familiar to Peter. In another mood he would have condemned the waste of space on the landing, but to-night he saw nothing but the girl, and, as she led the way into a small living-room, his concern was all for her.

She faced them.

"Well?" she said.

"We want to know what you and Murrison were doing in Bosverran," Bayles said aggressively.

"I don't know what you're talking about."

"Why did you go to Braddock's house?" he persisted. "What were you after?"

"You've forced your way in here by creating a disturbance on the doorstep. I've nothing to say to you. I'm not going to be bullied." She paused, probably to consider carefully her next words. They were deliberate when they came; they had the artificiality of something rehearsed.

"All you want is material for another of your infamous articles. You won't be happy till you ruin Britt and smash the movement. You'll print any lie that suits your purpose."

She turned away. A further flash of rage in Bayles made him grasp her by one shoulder and swing her round to face him.

"Who taught you that cant? Britt?" He was almost shouting. "I've done everything I can to protect you. I've held back things I should have used. I'm here now only because I want to keep you out of it."

"I can do without your protection. I can do without these empty threats, too. I don't know what Mr. Ackland has told you, but his friend would never let him bring in the police. You're in trouble already over this libel suit. You'd better be careful about the bluffs you use or you'll find yourself in a worse mess."

"Supposing you just answer a simple question. What were you doing in Braddock's house? Checking up on your hired thug? Making another search?"

She was rigid, facing him. She seemed cold and quite in command of herself, but her voice gave her away. The tremor was still there.

"I've no statement to make for publication," she said.

For a moment he stared. Then he shrugged. When he spoke you could see the effort he made to keep feeling out of his voice.

"Okay, Jess," he said. "I'm in the way. I'd better clear out and let Ackland talk to you. One of these days you'll see through Britt. I don't think it'll be long now."

He made a hopeless gesture of wiping things out as he turned away. From the doorway he added: "You know where to get me when you want me."

The words were addressed to the girl, but Peter thought they were for him as well. Bayles motioned him to stay where he was. He went, closing the door after him. The abruptness of it left Peter a little confused. He suspected a trick, that Bayles was out on the landing waiting to see what would happen, but a moment later the street door below was slammed again. The feeling of relief that came over him almost made him smile.

She had turned her head to watch the reporter go. She was still standing there, gazing at the closed door, but her expression had changed. The tremor that he had detected in her voice was now visible. She crumpled. She was sad. She became human. And Peter could not avoid noting that she was very lovely. Every time he saw her he found something new in her, but these things were intangibles, not to be catalogued.

For her the slam of the street door seemed to break a spell. She sat down on a small settee and pressed her hands to her face, covering her eyes.

Tears? He stared at her helplessly, trying to find the words he needed.

While he was still deliberating, she took her hands from her face and sat up straight, straight and dry-eyed. She had no difficulty in finding words.

"Why did you have to come here?" she demanded sharply and unexpectedly. "If Braddock has sold out to the *Gazette*, what more do you want? You've beaten us, and that's the end of it. Jim Bayles will publish your fake evidence. Before we can prove it's false, the damage will be done. People are always ready to believe the worst. What do you want now? A pat on the back? Or is your conscience beginning to trouble you?"

For a moment he stared at her. Quite suddenly a lot of the things that had happened became logical.

"Well?" she insisted.

He looked at her. "Shut up for a moment," he said coldly. "Shut up and listen."

Rather to his surprise she obeyed. Perhaps she had had no more to say.

Slowly and carefully he explained the history of his association with Braddock. "Now," he added, "I want to know where Braddock is. I feel I've some responsibility after what happened down there. If you can tell me he's safe, I'll wait till he turns up."

She was puzzled, but not contrite. Nor did she seem alarmed.

"How can I tell you?" she asked. "I don't know anything about his movements. Why should you be anxious?"

"He was supposed to go to Pero's Hotel. There's mail there for him; he hasn't been in to claim it."

"He must have gone to some other hotel. He's somewhere in London. I'm sure of that."

"I don't know." Peter shook his head. "There's another thing. I ordered a car to take him to Par. I telephoned from the Commercial Hotel and I believe Murrison heard me. When the driver called for Braddock, there was no one in the house."

"I can explain that. Murrison and Alfie drove him over to Par and saw him on to the train."

"Did he know at that time that they were after this so-called evidence?"

She hesitated. "Yes."

"And he allowed them to ship him off so that they could return to the house and make a search? Braddock may be a fool, but he's not an imbecile. It's incredible that he would go with them willingly."

"If he knew there was nothing for them to find in the house, why not?"

Peter considered this in an appreciable pause. "No," he decided. "That would make Murrison a bigger fool than I take him for. Braddock was coming to town to sell what you were all after. He must have had it in his pocket or his luggage. You can't ask me to believe that Murrison would help him to get away with it."

"Braddock had nothing with him."

"How do you know that?"

Once more the girl hesitated. "I know," she insisted.

"You mean that Braddock was searched as well as his house?"

"Can't you take my word for it?"

"Miss Trask, why not be frank?" Peter pulled up a chair facing her and sat down. "I'd like to take your word, to be on your side, but I can't make up my mind till I know the real facts."

He condemned himself for saying it, fearing that he was committing himself to too much. Her side meant Britt's side, and he was beginning to feel doubtful. If it were true that Britt was an innocent victim, he was behaving in a way that suggested guilt. Certainly he had prejudiced his position by trying to secure illegally something that he protested was false. To take a man from his house by force and search him was not a thing you could dismiss as merely ill-advised.

"He submitted willingly," the girl said. "He laughed at them. He told them they...."

Her voice was drowned out by a thought, a recollection, that sprang clamorously to his conscious mind. What had Murrison and his man been doing that afternoon in the winder-house of the disused clay-pit? He remembered the car crawling along the white road, and he knew that it was one of the roads you might take to Par. He saw the car driving on till it disappeared behind the great skytip, the malformed tip with the truncated shape that made a plateau-like step to the main cone. Next he was crossing the trestle bridge over the rails of the incline to find the fat man and his valet in the winder-house. That was after they had made the acquaintance of Braddock in the Green Dragon....

The girl on the settee came into sharp definition again. He saw her with a questioning look in her eyes, and he had to hide from her what was in his mind, to conceal if possible the agitation that sprang from his fear.

"What did you say?" he asked.

"He laughed at them."

"Braddock?"

"Of course, Braddock. He told them they could search him; they wouldn't find anything. He'd made sure of that. Afterwards ..."

He interrupted her. "Wait a minute. They took him to a winder-house up in the clay country, didn't they?"

"I don't know what a winder-house is. They stopped somewhere along the road."

"In all that rain. There was a terrible storm that night."

"I don't know. They may have gone through his things in the car. Afterwards they took him on to Par and put him on the London train."

"Then they went back to his house?"

"Yes. They kept his key. They said they'd send it to him."

"Later you borrowed it. Why did you go to the house?"

"I wanted to make sure they'd been thorough."

"They're always thorough, aren't they?" He paused, watching her closely. "They were quite thorough when they broke into my flat today."

Instead of the tell-tale reflex he expected, she showed surprise.

"Your flat?" Some implication of the act came to her slowly. She had been leaning back, a little relaxed. Now she jerked to an upright position, and he could see her growing more and more tense. The initial surprise was nothing to this developing apprehension of something gone wrong. Watching her closely, he saw the beginning of horror in her eyes. She sprang up, and he with her.

"What is it?" he asked quickly. "What are you thinking?"

She would not face him. "I don't know," she said. "It's confusing. I must find out where Braddock is. If I can tell you that he's safe, you'll be satisfied?"

"Yes, of course."

"I must find out at once. I'll have to go to the House."

"The Commons?"

"Yes." She moved towards her bedroom. "I shan't be long. Will you wait here for me?"

"I'll go with you."

"No. You mustn't do that."

He became more emphatic. "I'm going with you."

She came from the bedroom wearing hat and scarf; in the hall he held her coat for her. There was something very different now in her manner. The aloof and efficient secretary was no longer apparent. He saw a breaking down of reserve. She was appealing to him for help in some subtle way, without words, even without awareness. Either this, or he was creating something that did not exist, seeing her with a perception distorted by his growing fear about Braddock.

He saw her face in the hall mirror as she drew the ends of her belt into a loose loop. She met his gaze in the mirror and, startled, he saw that there were tears in her eyes.

She turned, and they were not a foot apart in the narrow hall, and the pendent light was harsh upon her face, revealing more in her eyes than the tears.

"I'm frightened," she said.

Her hands were raised in front of her, gripping her gloves, and her knuckles were white from the strain of her grip.

He touched her hands for a moment. They were colder than her gloves. He tried to think of something that would reassure her.

"It may not be so bad. Men like Braddock always manage somehow."

She shuddered and closed her eyes tightly, and he thought she was going to faint. Her hands gripping the gloves groped towards him, and he recalled that peculiar gesture of Braddock's, the hands thrust out in front of him. He grasped her by the elbows to steady her. She opened her eyes and blinked and gave a nervous shake of her shoulders.

"It may not be so bad."

He repeated the phrase. It was the more inane because he did not believe it could have any relieving effect. He knew that her fear was the same as his, and in him it was growing, becoming a conviction.

Chapter 11

They approached Parliament Square from the Embankment, walking the short distance from the flat. The massive shape of the Victoria Tower climbed into the darkness above the mist-dimmed street-lamps. The fog was thin and patchy, nothing to cause serious inconvenience to traffic, though it might demand wariness in driving. Even along the river it was not what you would call heavy. In shadowed places you had to keep a sharp look-out for pedestrians, but visibility for lights was not at all bad. As they went along Abingdon Street, Peter could see the mellow face of the clock in its high tower, and above it the gleam that told him the House was sitting. A taxi honked discreetly in Old Palace Yard, rolling away from the Peers' entrance in the direction of Millbank. The traffic rumbled ceaselessly round Parliament Square, but the Yard was quiet. Only a single horseman loomed through the fog, and he was on a pedestal.

"Wait here," Jessica Trask said. "I'll be as quick as I can."

Her tone was peremptory, but that was nervousness. She was on edge, shrinking from the coming encounter, yet there was no hesitation in her steps as she went towards the entrance to St. Stephen's Porch. She was in a hurry to resolve her doubts, though that resolution might be calamitous.

On the walk from the flat she had been in a hurry to fill out her version of the Braddock story, as if an immediate need was to have Peter understand everything fully. She was answering an unnamed charge, but her pleading was essentially for Britt. There was a curious fervour about it, as if her faith were threatened from within and she must at once persuade herself that all was well.

Britt was the victim of a sinister plot. Braddock knew how easily a reputation could be destroyed. He claimed to have found among the German archives a document incriminating Britt as a traitor. Braddock actually may have found something while working for Amgot; if so Britt knew it must be false, a forgery, the work of a personal enemy. Braddock had threatened to publish his document. Britt had laughed at him, knowing the charge could easily be refuted. Later, with the *Gazette* developing its campaign against him, Britt realised the document might damage him, because it was always difficult to overtake lying scandal with the truth. People who read the charge might not read the answer.

Unwisely, no doubt, but surely understandably, Britt had offered to buy the false document from Braddock. The answer was a demand for a preposterous figure, supported by a suggestion that the *Gazette* was interested. The impending libel action made it more desirable to clear up the matter, so Britt sent Murrison to Bosverran to treat with Braddock, and Jessica Trask, a very confidential secretary, had gone down to Cornwall, as stake-holder, as it were, to take possession of the forgery before any money was handed over.

Braddock had refused to negotiate when Murrison disclosed his purpose. He would, he asserted, deal only with Britt himself. Instead of reporting to Jessica, Murrison had decided to act on his own initiative. Zeal had carried him far beyond his instructions. Jessica had known nothing of the interference with Braddock and the vain search of the house until the next day. Murrison's excuse had been his belief that Braddock intended a deal with the *Gazette* in any case.

Peter went over the story as he paced in Old Palace Yard. It was feasible enough, as it had been received and retailed by Jessica Trask. It explained most of the happenings in Cornwall. It even explained the search of his own flat, for he had appeared to Murrison as the companion of Braddock. The big thing it did not explain was what had become of Braddock, and this deficiency posed the question of how much had been told to Jessica Trask. To what extent was she in the confidence of Britt; to what extent was she being abused in her loyalty? Wasn't it likely that Murrison's warrant had been to deal with Braddock, not merely to treat with him? Then, conceivably, Bayles was right, and Braddock was being softened up somewhere. In that case he was holding out, saying nothing, or there would have been no breaking and entering at Peter's flat that day.

There was an alternative possibility; that Braddock was saying nothing, but that the term of his silence would stretch to Judgment Day.

Peter pushed the thought away. You just didn't kill a goose of that sort. Not, at any rate, until it had led you to the place where it had laid the golden egg.

There was one thing he believed: Braddock had not carried the document with him when he left the house on the night of the storm. He might have posted it to himself in London, to Pero's, or to the G.P.O. He might have hidden it at Trevone Cottage and taken only a copy of it with him. But Murrison and Alfie had gone through the cottage very thoroughly, and if it had been there they would have found it. Unless it had been hidden in a very secret place; somewhere no one would think of looking.

Peter paused in his pacing and peered through the fog at Richard Coeur de Lion on his bronze horse, but that didn't help. It was rather difficult to imagine a place where no one would think of looking. If he had been Braddock with something to hide, he would have shoved it among the litter and paraphernalia on the kitchen table, but that would have been too simple for Braddock.

Pacing again, he began to turn over the details of his relationship with Braddock. A remembered word, an act, a gesture might give him the clue. He tried to focus on the peculiarities of Braddock, but there were so many.

Braddock discussing his books? Nothing. Braddock on a walk? Looking back, a scared man. Braddock in the garden? Nothing. Braddock shopping? A piece of hake.

Peter was approaching Richard once more. He saw a swirl of fog against the lights near the Peers' entrance. It was thickening a bit, but perhaps it was just a patch from the river. The fog drifted and spun and separated and trailed away over the Yard with an effect of passing clouds. Richard reached up into the murk with his raised sword.

Something moved at the base of the statue. A figure, a man in a mac. Halation from the lights in the Yard filtered thinly through the fog, and Richard and his horse were black masses projected upon a luminous screen. For an instant the man in the mac was visible against that same screen, a mist-shape, not quite solid, a silhouette cut from gossamer. One instant, and he drew back behind the pedestal.

Peter stopped and stared. People had been coming and going in the Yard, passing him; messengers, policemen, and peers no doubt. Absorbed, he had paid no attention, but this movement at the base of the statue arrested him. He had the impression of something furtive, and also of something familiar. He continued to stare at the spot for quite half a minute. Then he shrugged and turned and paced back towards the porch entrance. He was beginning to imagine things. The whole business was becoming too much for his weary nerves. If he didn't keep his head, he'd be seeing spies on every corner.

He paused at the end of his beat, wondering how much longer Jessica Trask was going to be. He paced towards the statue again, trying to proceed with his analysis of Braddock's words and actions, but as he came near to the great bronze he kept his gaze fixed on the fog-softened line of the low pedestal.

There was someone there all right. The vertical line was broken by the protruding curves of a hat, a head, a shoulder. The man was watching, believing, perhaps, that he was unobserved. He might be an innocent bystander, waiting for somebody, but there was at least a prima facie case for doubt; and for investigation.

Peter carried on along the established beat at his ambling gait, but then, instead of turning when he reached a point a few feet from the horse, continued on round the pedestal at a fast walk. His suspicion was confirmed, for he saw the man in hasty retreat towards Abingdon Street. He hesitated a moment, then started in pursuit. The mac, the hat, the man certainly seemed familiar.

He called after him: "Bayles! Wait for me! What the devil's your game?"

The figure in the mac dissolved in a swirl of fog beyond the Victoria Tower.

Peter pulled up. He certainly wasn't going to chase the fool to Millbank. He hurried back, thinking that the girl might have emerged. A rising irritation made him curse Bayles angrily. He had thought the man might have waited for him outside Jessica Trask's front door, but he had seen no sign of him on leaving with the girl. Now it seemed that the fellow had shadowed them down the street and along the Embankment to Westminster. It might be reasonable enough for him to keep away from Jessica Trask, but, with the girl inside the House somewhere, he could have come forward instead of playing hide-and-seek behind statues. And why had he retreated when challenged? Why, in heaven's name?

The fellow was as bad as Braddock himself. They were mad, all mad: the girl and Britt as well, and Murrison and Alfie. Now, Sanity Ackland was becoming infected. He glared at the dark mass of horse and rider and pedestal. He told himself he would have to keep calm, or Richard would be turning his bronze head to spy on him. He peered through the fog for the man in the mac, certain that he would return to continue the insane game. But this time, no doubt, he would choose some other vantage point. Perhaps he was across the way there, hovering between Westminster Abbey and the Chapter House.

Mad! Peter's heart was pumping faster than normal. He cursed himself as well as Bayles and the rest of them. What was he doing here in this wretched fog? Why didn't he go home, put his flat straight, and make himself comfortable? What was it to him whether Braddock had been kidnapped or not? Why should he wait for this crazy girl to confer with her totalitarian boss, if that was what he was? Much better if he went off and got himself a democratic drink in Whitehall. Confound Jessica Trask!

She came from the doorway, looking for him, and he hurried towards her. He had forgotten in the last minute how beautiful she was. It didn't matter how troubled and worried she might be, she was still beautiful.

Nothing she had heard from Britt had resolved her problem or abated her fear. Her husky voice had a dry tone of despair.

"Will you come with me?" she said. "He wants to see you."

He hesitated. Then he took her arm and went with her.

In the porch, talking to a young man who might have been another reporter, was Woodforde Bayles. Peter faltered. He had been quite sure that he had seen Bayles in the Yard; now he saw that he had been mistaken. The mac slung over the reporter's arm was much lighter in colour than the one worn by the watcher. Moreover, Bayles was at least a couple of inches taller than the man outside.

Peter was not pleased with himself as an observer. He would have to do better than this.

Jessica Trask walked on firmly when Bayles detained him. The reporter was grinning.

"I had a bet with myself you'd turn up in this joint," he said. "Not a bad guess, eh? I'd like to hear how you get on. I'll wait at the *Gazette* for you. Will you telephone when you've finished with the Führer?"

"Yes." He owed him that at least.

"How's Miss Muffet? Still in love with the spider?" Bayles grinned again. The grin said he had a lot of patience. He could wait till she came to her senses.

Peter nodded vaguely. He couldn't be bothered with Bayles at the moment. He had to think about Braddock.

The waiting girl led him up the steps and into St. Stephen's Hall.

"We're to wait for him here," she said.

Peter nodded again. He was near to something and it just wouldn't come to him. The long high-ceiled hall with its paintings and statues and red benches was a distraction. He was back in Braddock's kitchen, seeing the disordered jumble of things on the table, the shining stars made by splashes of solder.

"He only wants to explain to you. You see, it's so easy to destroy a man in his position, and a midget like Jim Bayles can tear him down. That is why he wants. . ."

She went on, talking in urgent whispers, her eyes strained with anxiety. The stars of solder formed constellations: Ursa Major and Aquarius and Leo. Where Orion should have been, there was the soldering iron. Braddock was a frightened man with a gun in his pocket. So he had got busy soldering something. . . an old saucepan. Is that what you did when you were frightened?

Drip . . . drip . . . drip.

But the overflow wasn't dripping then. It hadn't started until the day after the storm.

"It doesn't make sense," the girl said.

"What doesn't?"

She stared at him. "The *Gazette's* attitude. What else?"

"Braddock," he said. "Braddock doesn't make sense."

But she wasn't listening. She had drawn him farther along the hall and was looking forward intently. Britt was making his entrance.

There was a coming and going of members and officials as he appeared in the doorway. He paused on the steps to say a word to someone. It looked almost like a deliberate effect, a Parliamentary attitude, traditional. You might think of Caesar, thus, on the steps of the Forum – or Coriolanus would be the better figure. He would turn now, throw off his gown, and seek suffrage by his scars. "Look, sir, my wounds! I got them in my country's service . . . ."

Could it be that the person accosted snubbed him? Certainly the man hurried up the steps without a glance at Britt. The scene was ineffective. The leading actor had lost his grip. He looked round as if he needed a prompt. He picked out Jessica Trask and came on, Peter stared at him incredulously. He could scarcely believe that this was the dynamic prophet of the platform. Mass hypnotism must have blown him up to heroic proportions at that Kensington meeting, or he had since been reduced by physical shrinkage. He seemed inches shorter in stature, he had a paunch not previously in evidence, and the whole countenance of the camera studies had become a caricature. There were heavy bags under the eyes, the cheeks sagged, the lines of the thick-lipped mouth had a downward drag.

Jessica said: "This is Mr. Ackland."

Even to Mahomet the mountain was not in the habit of saying "How do you do?" Or it might have been the strain of events. Peter was prepared to make allowances. That was as well.

The great man nodded curtly.

"I've very little time," he announced. "There'll be a division on the second reading at any moment."

Another attitude, perhaps; with emphasis on the correct background. A few yards away, beyond closed doors, the chosen of the nation – or at least a quorum of them – were at their deliberations. Soon the division bells would ring, and the rest of them would come from the corridors, the social rooms, the library, and other places. The Ayes would pass to the right of the chair, the Noes to the left. The tellers would be busy in the lobbies and the second reading would be carried. Whichever way the sole representative of the N.L.P. voted, the second reading was bound to be carried, but it seemed he was determined to vote. He would get his name in Hansard, and no doubt that mattered.

He said: "Will you come this way?"

They went up the steps, crossed the octagonal Central Hall, and entered a corridor with more historical paintings and more red-upholstered benches. At one end a member was dictating letters to a secretary. Britt sought privacy at the other end. He waved Peter and the girl towards one of the benches and sat down between them.

"Miss Trask has told me about you, Mr. Ackland," he began. "I wish you had come straight to me instead of going to this Bayles fellow. I fear he may have planted some prejudice in your mind."

"I went to your office this morning. I left there full of prejudice."

"What do you mean?"

Peter told him. Britt disembarrassed himself of the information with a wave of his hand and a faint smile that managed to be rueful and patronising at the same time.

"Loyal workers are not always gifted with discretion, Mr. Ackland. Miss Dubetat has been worried about events at Bosverran. From one interpretation I might be made to appear in a bad light." He shrugged lightly. "There is another interpretation. I believe Miss Trask has told you that my agent exceeded his instructions. He had no orders from me to search Mr. Braddock's house."

"Did he have orders to search my flat?" Peter inquired, irritated by the pomposity of the man.

"That may have been a coincidence, a chance burglar."

"I find that difficult to believe."

"You will believe, I hope, that I am not responsible for it?"

"I suppose, then, you're not responsible for the man who's following me to-night?"

Britt was startled. So was the girl. She started to say something. Britt stopped her with a gesture.

"Just a moment, Miss Trask," he said. "What is this, Mr. Ackland? Are you sure of your facts?"

"Quite sure." Peter told of the incident in the Yard outside. "I've no doubt," he added, "I've been followed since I arrived in London this morning."

"You see!" The girl turned quickly to Britt. "I warned you about Murrison, I told you not to trust him. He's been working for . . . ."

"That's enough!" Britt said sharply. "We must think."

Peter filled in the interrupted sentence. Plainly what she saw was that Murrison had been working for himself. And Britt knew it. The colour of fear had come into his face. He had been hiding this fear, trying to combat it, but now it was taking possession. You could see it filling his eyes. You could hear it in his voice. He was knocking involuntarily with a clenched fist on his right knee, and the thud, thud, thud of it made an effect of syncopation with a tapping that came from beyond a stairway at the end of the corridor.

"This man," he said, "this man in Old Palace Yard, was he the one you saw with Murrison in Bosverran, the man he called his valet?"

"No." Peter was positive. "I never saw him before."

"They've brought in help," the girl said tonelessly.

Britt tried to frown. "Imagination," he said. "We mustn't let our imaginations . . . ."

"Just a moment," Peter broke in. "If Murrison is still exceeding his instructions, why don't you get hold of him and stop him? Personally, I don't like the idea of being followed round London. It's my opinion, Murrison could explain a good deal. At least, he may know where Braddock is."

There was silence for a moment. Then: "We don't know where

Murrison is," the girl said quietly.

This time the shock was for Peter. There was no movement from Britt. He was silent, sagging on the bench as if the fear that was paralysing his will was also attacking his spine.

The sound from beyond the stairway seemed louder.

Clack ... clack ... clack ...

It was like a metronome, but what would a metronome be doing at Westminster? More likely it was an object swinging against a door or panel of wood. The place was draughty.

The girl said: "It's my opinion Murrison has gone back to Bosverran. Braddock's house is shut up. He could search it daily if he wanted to. No one would be the wiser. He has suspected the house all the time. He'll pull it to pieces. He'll search till he finds what he wants. Then you'll see, Mr. Britt. You'll see I was right. He'll make you pay."

Peter rose from the bench. "It's time I went to the police," he stated. "If you don't know where Braddock or Murrison is, it's high time."

"No!" Britt raised his voice, and the note of fear was near to panic. "Don't bring in the police. They must be kept out of it at all costs."

"Why?" Jessica Trask asked. "We've done all we can do. We've done too much, considering everything. If the fake evidence turns up, you'll have to face it and prove it false. It was a mistake not to face it from the first. The longer we delay now, the worse it will be. Mr. Ackland's right. It's high time the police were told."

"No!" The panic was unmistakable. Britt reached out a hand and caught Peter's sleeve. "No," he repeated. "Not while there's a chance."

"Chance of what?" The girl's voice rang out sharply. The secretary at the other end of the corridor looked round.

"Don't raise your voice. Please don't raise your voice." Command had gone from Britt. He was pleading. "You can see for yourself what chance." He turned to Ackland, "You can see, can't you? Murrison hasn't found anything. If he had, your flat wouldn't have been searched. You wouldn't have been followed. You must help me. I'll pay you well. I'd have paid Braddock if he had been reasonable."

Clack ... clack ... clack....

That infernal tapping had started again. Irritating. Peter pulled his sleeve from Britt's grasp. He had a vision of Braddock, pigeon-toed, at the kitchen table, solder in one hand, the hot iron in the other. The vision was inconvenient because he was behind Braddock. He couldn't see what the man was soldering.

"The thing's in that house," Britt said. "He has hidden it somewhere. You know the house, Ackland. You must have some idea where it might be. If you would think . . . Braddock may have said something, dropped a hint. You're the one man who could find it for me. That's the plan. You see, don't you? Once Murrison and his clique are beaten, they'll let Braddock go. They've got him somewhere. It's the only explanation."

Peter's mind flicked over to the lonely winder-house on the edge of the disused clay-pit. He saw the man Alfie staring at the motor from the driving platform, saw the fat Murrison in the doorway.

But it was out of the question. They couldn't keep a prisoner in that shed. It might be inspected at any time. It would be on the list of the maintenance man. Or Captain Hicks might look in to make sure that everything was all right. It was important to keep the machinery in order for a possible resumption of work. There were wagons loaded with waste and rubble, waiting to be drawn up the incline to the skytip. Any day a man might be sent to the winder-house to attend to them.

Yet it might be argued that Murrison, knowing nothing of these things, had used the winder-house for his purpose. Peter was only too well aware that his own knowledge was inexact; that so far as he really knew, none of the clay-pit workers might go near the place for weeks, or even months.

Britt had gone on talking, urging, pleading. Here, in this moment, slumped down on the red bench under the high-keyed painting of a former patriot on his way to the chopping block, this leader of patriots proceeded to another kind of dissolution. Perhaps the certainty of Murrison's treachery had pricked his last hope. He could keep face no longer, but in his fear he no longer cared.

"I'll pay you well." He kept on repeating that. "You must go back to Braddock's house and search. You must find the thing for me. You must think where it is, and find it. Look! There's time." He raised his left wrist so that Peter could see the watch on it.

"Twenty past eight. You can catch the night train from Paddington." He swivelled towards Jessica Trask with an effort. "What time is the train?"

"Nine-fifty." The girl's voice was dead. She stared at the opposite wall.

Clack . . . clack . . . clack. . . .

It recalled the rhythm of the drip from the waste-pipe at Trevone Cottage. It suggested the swinging of a wooden acorn at the end of a blind-cord.

"You hear, Ackland? Nine-fifty from Paddington. You needn't worry about money. I'll pay you well."

Drip . . . drip . . . drip. . . .

The drops formed, fell from the waste-pipe, and splashed in the middle of the garden path.

"How much will you pay?" Peter asked.

Jessica Trask jerked her head up to look at him. If Peter had seen the look he might have felt flattered by her incredulity. Whatever else she had thought of him, she had not thought this.

"I offered Braddock a hundred," Britt said. "It's worth that to me not to have any fuss."

"Braddock thought it was worth more, didn't he?"

"Two hundred, then. I'll pay you two hundred."

Peter stood in front of the man, looking down at him, watching every flicker in the heavy, crumpling face. Two hundred pounds seem to bear no relation to the amount of fear. Peter wanted to know the true value. Or it might be that his real purpose was to show the girl the true value. He glanced at her, then faced Britt again.

"It isn't enough," he said.

"You know where it is," Britt claimed excitedly. "You've known all along. Bring it to me and I'll give you three hundred. Four, five hundred."

"You mustn't jump to conclusions, Mr. Britt."

But Britt did not hear the words. He heard only the sound of evasion, of rejection.

"All right," he said. "Let's talk business. How much to you want? A thousand?"

"I've nothing to sell," Peter answered.

"You think you've got me, don't you?" Britt hoisted himself on to his feet and grasped Peter's sleeve again. "You've planned it together, you and Braddock. You fixed it so that you could carry on if anything happened to him. All right. I'm beaten. I'll pay you what Braddock asked."

"Well?"

"You know how much. Five thousand."

The girl gazed at the man with a look in her eyes that might have been horror or dismay, or both. The revelation was complete. She must see him as Bayles had described him, or perhaps as something worse. He had not even the strength to pretend any more. The image was crumbling before her eyes.

"You're mistaken. I can't help you." Peter drew back a step, but Britt would not relinquish the grip on his sleeve. He saw in Peter his last hope, and he must cling to it.

"Bring me the letter," he begged. "I'll pay whatever you ask, as much as I can raise. What happens to me doesn't matter, but I can't let the movement down."

"When I find Braddock, I'll tell him."

"Never mind about Braddock. Get on that night train. You must stop Murrison. You must."

The tapping sound came again, and was translated into the drip of water from the waste-pipe. Images raced quickly through his mind, blurring, fading, coming back: the kitchen table, Braddock, the cistern, the ripped upholstery, the stars of solder, the dripping water, the acorn swinging like a pendulum on its cord. Cord? The images spun away, fading into a thin fog, and he was focusing on a length of blind-cord. How much did a length of blind-cord shrink when you soaked it in water?

The question blew out into immense significance as he shaped it and vaguely answered it for himself. Such close-woven cord would shrink a little at least; a lot, perhaps. Enough, certainly. Enough to depress slightly the ball-float of a cistern and cause water to drip from the waste-pipe.

One place you wouldn't think of searching for a letter was in a tank of water. Not, at any rate, if you were a bungler like Murrison. Braddock had made his treasure safe enough. Now it was even safer. The cord, the one thing that might have led to its discovery, was cut.

Peter had a sudden overwhelming feeling of relief. This document or letter that they were all after was virtually in his hands. It would lie at the bottom of the cistern till he claimed it. Or until Braddock returned. Tomorrow he could secure it, if he wished. He could sell it to Britt for five or ten thousand. He could give it to Woodforde Bayles. He could tear it up, or burn it. Meanwhile he must be careful. The girl was staring at him curiously, as if she could divine something of what was passing through his mind.

He said, in a casual tone: "How long is it since you lost touch with Murrison?"

The girl answered. "He was in London yesterday afternoon. He didn't return to his flat last night."

"What makes you think he went back to Bosverran?"

"I don't know. That man of his, Alfie, stayed in Cornwall."

"I thought you all came up together in the Austin."

"No." She shook her head. "Alfie drove us to Liskeard. He said he was going back to Bodmin. It looks to me as if he and Murrison had something planned."

"It's clear enough," Britt interposed eagerly. "They've got Braddock out there. Someone had to stay to look after him. If you don't catch the night train, Ackland, you'll be too late. Between them they'll break Braddock down. They'll get to the house before you. You owe it to Braddock to hurry. I've told you I'll pay whatever you ask. That ought to be enough for you. Here." He fumbled with a wallet and produced a sheaf of five-pound notes. "Here's money to go on with."

"Put it away", Peter told him. "You'll have to get it out of your head that I'm Braddock's accomplice. I'm not. He told me nothing about this letter that's so valuable to you. But if there's going to be any more interference with his house, I ought to be out there to stop it. If I find the letter, I'll decide what I'll do with it when I've read it."

The clamour of a bell broke in on the last sentence. Britt raised his voice against the noise. "What did you say?" he asked.

"I'll decide when I've read it."

The ringing went on, stopped, started again. The member at the far end of the corridor deserted his secretary hastily.

Britt said: "You'll decide . . ."

He backed towards the bench and sat down. He seemed exhausted. He lifted a hand and pressed hard with his fingers on his brow. Peter was conscious of a stir in the Central Hall, a shuttling of people. Messengers called something in a tone of dry warning.

Jessica Trask spoke, pitching her voice high enough to cut through the ringing.

"Mr. Britt! The division bell!"

Two members came up the stairs to the corridor and passed urgently towards the House.

"Mr. Britt! They're taking the division."

He would not hear her. He made an impatient gesture of dismissal. "That's all," he told her. "You may go home. That's all."

She turned towards Peter appealingly.

"Come on," Peter said. "I want to talk to you."

He felt the beginning of a headache. He was aware of more momentary breaks in the ringing, one more, two more. Now the sound was overpowering, as if a hundred bells were hammering, splitting his mind into particles. Voices pierced the din. "Division! Division! Division!" More people hurried along the corridor and crowded in the Central Hall. "Division!"

Suddenly he realised that he was spent, mentally and physically. He looked at Britt in weariness. He saw time running towards an end for the man who could not rise from the red bench, and time, in Peter's vision, was the falling of sand in a minute glass. For all he knew, there might be such an instrument on the table of the House to set a period to this summons. It was there in his mind, at any rate, and the sand glistened as it piled its little heap within its glass bulb – a miniature skytip in a crystal chamber.

When he looked at Britt he saw dejection, despair hopelessness. The little hope that had risen had ebbed away, and once more he knew that things were as bad as they could be. He was sorry for the girl. He ought to go to the police at once. He ought to cross over to Whitehall, and go straight to Scotland Yard; but he was sorry for her. He had to make sure that there was nothing in the cistern to smash her belief in her brother. There was enough for her to face in the end of the idol Britt.

The clamour went on.

He was angry. He wanted to take hold of the girl and shake her. It was because of her that he had to plunge on into more irrational behaviour, to do things he wouldn't have dreamed of doing a week ago.

"Come on!" he shouted at her above the din.

She obeyed. She left Britt and followed him. He looked back from the end of the corridor, and at that instant the ringing stopped. The last grain of sand had fallen in the glass, the legislators had assembled, and in the chamber the traditional order was being given to lock the doors.

The Central Hall was empty, except for the attendants and a few visitors left in suspense. The silence seemed startling, more intense because of the noise that had ended. In such a hush you might listen for the voice of the Speaker putting the question to the House, yet no murmur would reach you from beyond the locked doors. Only if you knew the ritual could you hear the voice.

Britt sat motionless on the red bench.

"The Ayes will pass to the right of the Chair, the Noes to the left."

But it was too late for Mr. Britt. He would not get his name in Hansard to-night. That would come later.

Chapter 12

THE fog was thinner. As soon as he was outside, Peter had a good look to the right, to the left, and across the way. He walked round the statue of Coeur de Lion, went on as far as the Victoria Tower Gardens, then hurried back to rejoin Jessica Trask.

"Why did you do that?" she asked indifferently. "You can't expect to surprise the man a second time."

"I don't know," he answered. "I may have been wrong the first time. It's quite possible the fellow I saw was just waiting for somebody . . . I'd better find a taxi and take you home."

"I can't bear the thought of home," she answered. "Not yet. If you're going down to Cornwall to-night, let me come to Paddington with you."

All his anger had gone with the last vibration of the bells. The knowledge he had placed her so much in his hands. He even felt a little tender towards her, so it was not unpleasing to think of her turning towards him. He wondered how he could respond; how he could give her a sign that she should trust him.

He said: "I'm hungry. I must get a sandwich."

They crossed Bridge Street, and he took her into the first bar he saw. He bought her brandy and made her drink it. She sat with him at a table while he ate sandwiches, but would eat nothing herself. She looked white and strained. She was hurt and silent, and his concern for her grew. She did not talk until they had reached Paddington, and he had bought a return ticket to Bosverran Road. Then, when they were out in the main hall, she challenged him.

"You know where the letter is, don't you?"

"I'm not sure." He would not commit himself wholly. "I've an idea, that's all. I may be wrong."

"If you find it. . . ." She checked. "No. I won't ask. You'll have to be the judge."

"What's in the thing?"

"I don't know. Mr. Britt had a copy from Braddock. He destroyed it. He said the original must be a forgery."

"You still believe that?"

"I don't know."

"Do you think he would offer all that money for a fake? Would he get in a panic over something he could prove was false?"

"I don't know."

"You saw the state he was in to-night? Doesn't that make it clear to you?"

She began to cry, and there was nothing he could say to comfort her. A motor luggage-truck bore down on them, with warning bell clanging. He grasped her by one arm and drew her out of the way, behind the structure of the arrival indicator. He continued to hold her arm, as though she were a distressed child. He knew that she was suffering one of the agonising disillusionments of childhood, and that the capacity for self-torture of the adult might make it intolerable. The pressure of his fingers through her sleeve would tell her that at least she was not alone.

Another motor truck went trundling past them, piled high with luggage. A train came in. Passengers debouched from the arrival platform, and flowed over the main hall in many streams, coursing towards taxis and tubes, with here and there some little swirls and eddies of indecision.

A man with a small valise stopped to ask a question.

"Excuse me. What's the quickest way to get to Liverpool Street?"

"Try the Underground," Peter advised him.

The man went off in the wrong direction, checked, and turned. A man in a brown mac.

Jessica fumbled in her handbag, seeking a handkerchief.

"I'm sorry," she said.

The hall was less crowded now. They walked and re-walked the space between the arrival indicator and the rows of benches. People were sitting on the benches, vague shapes with blank faces, except one in the third row at the train-gate end: a man in a brown mac.

A giant voice, dehumanised by amplifiers, reverberated under the high glazed roof, pitching a strident, grasshopper noise against the screaming safety valve of a locomotive.

Multiple clock-faces made a chorus of time. Nine-fifteen.

"There's nothing to wait for," Peter said. "Don't you think you should go home now?"

She touched his arm in appeal against dismissal. "I've been trying to tell you. After all, we're strangers and it isn't so easy, especially when it sounds so … I don't know. It's a matter of trust. I feel I can trust you."

"Do you?"

"I know why you led him on about the money. You wanted me to see him as you see him."

Through the thin drift of fog under the roof he peered at one clock-face, then at another. He saw the minute hand of the second clock jump forward. His gaze shifted to a third clock and focused on the longer hand.

"How do you know I won't take his price?" He heard in his voice the hard, acid accent of the shrewd, calculating man, sharp to pick up a windfall, not at all particular about the source of the breeze.

"I know." The simple affirmation was a blade to transfix him. He knew her eyes were on him, waiting for him to turn his head, but he was afraid to face her. The black hand of the clock gave an epileptic jerk.

"It's a question of who's right," she went on. "I've helped him for a long time. You see, I know quite a lot about him."

"All I know is what he has shown me."

"You're just …" She hesitated, considering her words. "Just an observer from outside. You don't hate him as some people do. You can judge him fairly."

"What can I say when I see a man in such a panic, offering me thousands for something he says is false? Do *you* still think it's false?"

"It could be."

"You didn't think so when we left him at the House."

"I've had time to consider. I'm not trying to persuade you. I want you to be fair. That's all. He's been under a lot of strain. People have been trying to destroy what he's done. Not ordinary people. Three nights ago a gang tried to beat him up. They might have killed him if it hadn't been for the police. He's no coward, but a man doesn't have to be a coward to panic. He doesn't have to be guilty either, especially not when people he has trusted turn against him."

"We don't know what's in this letter of Braddock's. We'd better wait."

"I want you to be fair," she repeated.

"I'll be fair." He hesitated. "I think I'd better see about my seat."

The train was standing at the platform. He hoped she would go now, but she stayed with him. There weren't many people travelling and well forward he found an empty compartment, dropped his hat and raincoat in a corner seat, and returned to the platform where she was waiting.

She wrote down her address and telephone number. She wanted him to telephone as soon as he had news. She would await his judgment, confident he would be just.

Confident, but she carried on the argument. There was the familiar point about the havoc publicity could cause, the impossibility of overtaking a lie with the truth. The damage done could be irreparable, so a man might buy himself out of a frame-up, might pay everything he had to save his life's work from ruin.

Standing there on the platform they were like sad lovers clinging to the last moments before separation. Late-comers were hurrying past them and a porter ran with a missing bag.

Tears sprang to her eyes again. He saw her in doubt once more, and knew that all the arguments and pleading with which she had been trying to convince herself were already failing her. New doubts kept rising, doubts of herself. She made one more plea for fairness.

"I've been unfair myself," she confessed. "Especially to Jim Bayles. He always warned me . . ."

It might have been the final abandonment of the illusion.

Coming between them, the giant voice of the station crackled the departure warning through the amplifiers.

"Bayles!" Peter exclaimed sharply. "I forgot. He's waiting at the office to hear from me. I don't like to ask you to do something you'd hate. . . ."

"I'll 'phone him at once." She seemed to catch eagerly at the suggestion, so eagerly that some vague misgivings caught at him.

"Tell him I've gone down to Cornwall. I'll let him know if there's any news. Tell him anything."

He was hurrying towards the train, and she with him. The minute hand of the platform clock jerked to the moment of departure. Doors slammed and people moved to windows. He pressed her arm. He wanted to say something cheerful, but couldn't. He leaned out, watching her, as the train started and gathered speed, flowing out into the thin fog. She was walking quickly along the platform and did not turn to look back. He saw her raise her handbag and open it, and he knew she was looking for pennies for the telephone.

The image of her was with him long after she was out of sight, and for a while he continued to stand at the window, fixed there by an uneasy feeling of loss.

He was alone in the compartment; but the train couldn't have been far past the coal depots of Westbourne Park when a man came along the corridor and looked in. He had actually started to slide back the door when he changed his mind and went on. The next compartment apparently suited him better. At least the door noises indicated that he had entered it. A man in a brown mac.

Outside, lights leaped past the window. Others wheeled slowly and dully in the middle distance. Then there was a thick patch of fog, obscuring everything beyond the track-side.

Peter settled himself in his corner. He was very tired and it was good to stretch out. Then weariness clogged thought, swirling over his mind like the fog coming up from the river. A thick patch obliterated everything. He drifted into a kind of stupor that was the next thing to sleep. Then the fog cleared, dispersed suddenly by an explosion of thought.

A man in a brown mac!

He sat up with a startled, almost convulsive movement. He wheeled towards the door, as if he feared to encounter the gaze of the man in the mac through the glass panel. There was no one in the corridor. He got up, slid back the door, and had a look. No one. The first quiet flowing motion of the train had developed into a roaring, pounding drive. It had a tearing urgency, ripping out into the country, throwing off the untidy skirts of London.

Looking into the empty corridor, he had an overwhelming sense of isolation. There was no train. There was only this hurtling, swaying coach, himself, and the man in the next compartment.

When he closed the door and sat down again, he was conscious that his heart was pumping violently. His mind leaped at wild, irrational thoughts. The menace might approach at any moment. He would be defenceless against an armed man. Except that he could reach up and pull down the communication chain and stop the train.

He stared at the few inches of chain. He wondered if he would have to give it a hard tug or whether it would be responsive to a light touch. All the years he had travelled on trains, no one had ever pulled the thing. He had forgotten that it existed. But it was there all right, with its warning tag. "*To Stop the Train in Case of Emergency Pull Down the Chain. Penalty for Improper Use, £5.*"

The chain looked tarnished – it might be defective, eaten away by corrosion. One tug might break it. . . .

He got up to examine it, to make sure.

The door behind him screamed open. The sound had a threatening violence. At the moment of its impact he was paralysed. He could not raise a hand nor turn.

"Ticket, please!"

His knees bent, his body sagged down. Relief came as suction follows blast. Painful. His finger tips had tingling points of pain as they touched the smooth leather of his wallet.

"Change at Par."

He snatched at something better than the alarm signal. "I suppose there's no chance of a sleeper."

"I'm afraid not, sir. We were fully booked to-night. Not a single cancellation." The official returned the snipped ticket. "Thank you, sir."

In a sleeper he would have been safe. He could have locked the door.

He looked out into the corridor again. He heard the click of the ticket-punch in the next compartment, and the train official said: "Change at Par, sir."

That might have been expected. The man had followed him from Westminster to Paddington. Once at the station, he would have known the programme, where to book to.

Of course, change at Par . . . .

The fellow had come through the train in search of his quarry, so he couldn't have been on the job of watching all the time. Knowing that Peter would use the nine-fifty, he had taken time off for food and drink. Or, more likely, he had used the interval to get in touch with accomplices, to report his movements, to warn Murrison by telephone.

Explanations, theories, fantasies shuttled through Peter's mind. He waited till the ticket-collector had gone on, then he went along the corridor to the lavatory at the end of the car so that he might examine his neighbour in passing. It was the man in the brown mac all right, and he had the compartment to himself. He was sitting up in a corner reading a book, and the coat was spread over his knees like a travelling-rug.

Coming back, Peter was slower, more deliberate in his inspection. First, he observed that there was no luggage on the rack. Then chance favoured him. A lurch of the train threw him heavily against the door of the compartment, and the man looked up. He had a mild, almost gentle face. He looked intelligent and scholarly. He might be a don, or the curator of a museum. He was, for his appearance, the last man you would associate with a group of political gangsters. He glanced incuriously through his reading spectacles at the passenger who had thudded against the door, then turned again to his book.

Peter went into his own compartment rubbing a bruised shoulder but feeling better. That type of brown mac was offered in thousands, probably in tens of thousands, to a population of millions. Why, damn it all, he was wearing exactly the same kind of thing himself, and there it was, on the rack above his head. The man next door had no visible luggage, but did that make him a criminal? Peter himself had no luggage, yet his journey was quite lawful. The man might have mountains of luggage in the van. Or he might be travelling between a town flat and a country cottage, and have no need of luggage. And, surely to goodness, the unfortunate man was entitled to change at Par if his destination required it? Bosverran Road was only one of several stations on the spur line.

"*To Stop the Train . . . Penalty for Improper Use . . .*"

Peter looked at the thing in disgust; and was shaken by the fresh realisation of the ease with which he fell a victim to his own imagination. It was appalling. His mind must be splitting up, falling to bits. He did not know what to think any longer. All that he had thought in the last few hours seemed absurd. He was convinced now that the man behind the statue in Old Palace Yard had been an innocent bystander. He must try to get back to reality.

But he'd been right about Braddock!

He leapt to his feet.

He had no reason for the action except that his thoughts would not let him sit still It was a fine idea that doctor had had, sending him to Cornwall, sending him into this mess. A nice, quiet psychiatric ward wouldn't have been nearly as restful.

Now he was cooped up in a swaying, lurching, terrifying night train, cooped up with nothing to do. He hadn't a book to read like the museum curator next door. He hadn't even bought an evening paper. And he could never sleep on a train. Never.

He put a cigarette in his mouth and held his last match to it. The train lurched and the match went out. He cursed. He opened the door and walked in the corridor, the other way this time. There were people in all the compartments. Some were reading; others had put the lights out. It was still a bit foggy outside; but, of course, they hadn't yet cleared the Thames country, and most likely it would be foggy all across Berkshire.

The expedition wasn't interesting. He lurched and reeled back along the corridor. The curator was still reading his book. He had opened his door, and he looked up as Peter took another look at him. Peter halted, and spoke through the doorway.

"I'm sorry to trouble you, but could you oblige with a light? I've used my last match."

The curator took off his glasses. "I believe I have a box. Ah, yes. Help yourself to some."

His voice was dry, acid, abrupt. There was something in it that contradicted the mild, almost benign cast of the face, and, observed more closely, the eyes were cold.

"Thanks." Peter produced his cigarette-case. "Will you have a cigarette?"

"No, thank you. I don't smoke." The curator smiled. It was an unprepossessing smile, perhaps because it got no endorsement from the eyes. They had a curious intensity, now that they reached out beyond the focal length of the glasses. Not an easy man to argue with, whatever his subject.

Peter smiled back at him. He felt encouraged to borrow a discarded evening paper on the seat, and was told it was his, to do with as he wished. "I'm afraid there's nothing new in it," the curator added. "Just throw it away when you've finished."

He probably meant there was nothing new in it about, say, the wall paintings in the Lascaux cave, or the ritual vessels of the Aztecs.

Peter apologised for his intrusion and returned to his compartment. Whether or not there was anything in the paper he couldn't decide. He read without understanding. He read words that had no continuity. Vague images began to fade even as they formed in his mind. The T.U.C. had come to some decision about wages, a woman had burst into flames in Wolverhampton, a man had disappeared. A man had.... No, it wasn't Braddock.

The curator had tried to do the crossword puzzle and given up. He had pencilled in three words and made several erasures. Apparently he had failed over a four letter national emblem beginning with 'L'. But the minds of scholars sometimes were like that. They couldn't see a leek for a lily, not even when an obvious auk supplied the last letter.

Peter finished the puzzle in three minutes, then studied, in the cookery column, the principles of hare-jugging. He tried to think if there was anything he disliked more than jugged hare, but there were subtleties in the problem, and it was too much for him. He drifted away into a reverie, the paper fell to the floor, he dozed, started awake, switched off the lights, dozed again.

He came back to consciousness with a sudden start, to a swift apprehension of silence. The train had stopped. In the moment of shock he had the thought that he had pulled the alarm signal in his sleep. Then he heard the tread of heavy boots and the trundling of a truck along a paved platform. They were at Bristol, in Temple Meads station.

Bristol? He groped in a daze, feeling his way back through time and space. He looked at his watch. Fifteen minutes to two.

There were far-away sounds, and the train started again, turning southward. The noise of it was a comfort restored. No longer was it harsh and terrifying. It soothed. Peter stretched and turned and settled himself along the seat, and slept again, unaware of further stops until Plymouth was reached. He thought he would take a turn on the platform, see if he could get a cup of tea, but he was too late. As soon as he was out of the coach, he had to get back in again.

He felt grimy with train dust. He sluiced his face with cold water in the lavatory, and used a handkerchief for towel. He seemed to be the only one awake in the car. The curator was sleeping; at least, his compartment was in darkness, with blinds pulled down.

Peter stood in the corridor as the train rumbled over Saltash Bridge. The night showed no sign of ending. It was black, with a heavy overcast, but there was no fog. The lights of ships on the Tamar and in the port were brilliant.

Half-past five, or a few minutes later. They were in Cornwall now, over the river. They had run into a deeper night, without a single gleam to prick the blackness. He stayed in the corridor, smoking a cigarette. By the time it was done, a few people were stirring. Liskeard. One or two alighted. Next stop Par.

Time dragged. In the night ahead you could hear the locomotive panting asthmatically. Peter went back to his seat. No luggage to bother about. It was the way to travel all right. He looked out of the window. A distant light came in sight. It divided, multiplied. He went to the end of the corridor and waited, ready to step out.

The train slowed and halted. A number of people tumbled out and started to fuss over bags and boxes. Par was a handful of dim lights in the night. Peter walked westward along the platform till he came to the end of it, till he was as far from the little disturbance of passengers as he could get. It was a relief to achieve this isolation after the cooped-up torment of the long journey. He felt he could think again. Certainly he could breathe, and he breathed deeply, standing on the end of his little promontory.

It was cold; very cold for Cornwall. He watched the main-line train proceed on its journey. He watched till its lights had disappeared, and there was only a purring in the night to tell of its progress towards Penzance. Then it was time to take a seat on the branch line train.

He found an empty compartment, but this time he was not to remain in sole possession. Just before the train started, the curator stepped in.

Of course, he, too, had been told to change at Par. Peter had forgotten the man, and it seemed that he, too, had been forgotten. Perhaps the curator was absentminded, not very observant of casual intruders who borrowed matches and newspaper. He gave no sign that he had ever seen Peter before, and to Peter's polite good-morning he returned an echo that was no more than the coldest acknowledgement.

Perhaps he was not at his best in the chill hour before the Cornish dawn. He loosened the belt of his brown mac, sat down in the opposite corner, and, as the train made a jolting start, hauled out his book, and began to read.

Peter was glad of it. He didn't want to make conversation. Now that he was so near to Bosverran again, he had too much on his mind. He was stimulated by the thought that he was close in time to the solution of a riddle; but there were other thoughts that depressed him. He was worried about Jessica Trask, fearful that her loyalty to Britt might cause her more anguish than she had yet faced.

On the other hand, when she came to her senses, she would undoubtedly make up her quarrel with Woodforde Bayles, and that might lead her into even worse trouble. The quarrel, of course, had broken up a beautiful friendship, but Bayles, in his continued concern for her, had shown that his feelings were deep. And the girl herself? Guilt alone would hurry her to the inevitable end, and it was rather a pity, because this fellow Bayles – he really wasn't right for her. It was gravely to be doubted whether he could make her happy. He was a year or two too old to begin with.

Peter shrugged. It was nothing to him what they did. Only he rather feared he had made a mistake in asking her to telephone Bayles on his behalf. That had given Bayles an opportunity which he might have been quick to grasp. Already they might be reconciled. With her temperament, in her present distress, she would be only too ready to weep on his shoulder. She was lonely. She needed comfort and guidance. Not that the divorced Mr. Ackland was a candidate for the post of comforter and guide. Once this business of the letter was cleared up, he had no intention of ever seeing her again. One wife had been enough. Quite enough. . . .

He found the curator's curious eyes gazing at him over the top of his book, but they dropped quickly to the printed page.

Peter thought this a little strange. He wondered if he had been grimacing at his own thoughts, putting on a show. He watched the man in the opposite corner. The curator had a way of holding the book so that only the top of his brow was visible above it. Peter could see the title of the book quite clearly. It was *The Psychology of Reasoning.*

He waited, watching. He was sure that presently the book would be lowered to enable the reader to take another look over the top of it. He was right.

Caught out, the curator put the volume on the seat, removed his glasses, and switched on his dehumanised smile.

He said: "Pardon me. I've been puzzling over the familiarity of your face. Haven't we met somewhere?"

"I borrowed a match on the train last night. Don't you remember?"

"Of course! How stupid of me!" The curator laughed at himself quite elaborately. "I was under the impression that you had got off at Exeter. That is, I thought the young man who borrowed the match got off at Exeter. Are you going on to Newquay?"

"No. Only as far as Bosverran Road."

"A coincidence." The curator smiled frostily. "Except that there is no such thing as a coincidence. I am getting off at Bosverran Road myself. Do you live in the neighbourhood? I would have taken you for a Londoner."

"I'm staying outside Bosverran for a few weeks."

"Ah, then I'll be able to give you a lift in the car. Unless, of course, you're having someone meet you. I live beyond Bosverran, on the Bodmin side."

"You're very kind, but I can't think of putting you out."

"My dear young man, you're not putting me out. I shall be glad of the company. I'll drop you in the town, and you may make your own way from there."

Afterwards, Peter was to think that the whole thing had been managed rather cleverly. Or had he been stupid, swallowing so readily the prepared suggestion of studious preoccupation and myopic groping? Everything conformed so neatly to his own wretched fantasies about the man that he was completely off guard. At the time he was grateful. A lift was an unexpected blessing. Without it, he would have had to find a telephone and get Ben Stevens out of bed.

The first chink in a night that had seemed impregnable appeared as the train neared the halt, a thin smudge of muddy grey light that defined a segment of flat skyline in the south-east.

"Bleak," said the curator. "But to be preferred, no doubt, to London under fog. Do you not think so?"

The smile seemed more detached than ever. The eyes looked through the close-fitting holes of a mask.

Curious fellow. Absent-minded. When the train pulled up, he was quite unaware that this was his destination. He realised it only when

Peter got up and opened the door.

Peter had misgivings. He doubted if there would be any car waiting in the roadway. If anyone was going to provide a lift, he felt that he would have to do it.

The old porter came along the platform to collect their tickets. The train was off again before he reached them.

Peter was right. There was no car, but the curator was undismayed.

"It's just like that man of mine," he said. "Never wants to get out of bed in the morning. Let's start along the road, shall we? He's bound to be on the way. Probably meet us before we've gone a hundred yards."

The chink in the south-east was widening and reaching up, giving a faint, misty radiance to the overcast. At first you could see only the dull smear of the road, then nearby trees stood out dimly.

They must have gone more than a hundred yards, but there was no sign of any car coming along the road. Peter looked back towards the string of lights that marked the station. They might have been pinholes in a black screen; a screen with a candle behind it. Suddenly the candle was puffed out, and the screen had an unbroken opacity. Imagination, of course, but he could have sworn he heard the click of the switch.

Imagination was too fond of playing tricks. The fact was, the old porter had turned off the lights and gone home to get a cup of tea. Imagination made the fact into an act of obliteration. The station was gone, it was wiped out, it had never existed, and with it had gone the railway line. In this mood you might doubt that it ever had existed. A moment ago you could hear the train purring in the distance, running westward with the retreating night. Now there was no sound, nothing. He was alone with this stranger in a dead world, and, in the bleak creeping of the grey light from the south-east, their brown macs were like the uniforms of ghosts.

"Might as well carry on," the curator said. "It's warmer to keep walking, anyway."

Against the spread of greyness the dead world began to reveal its contours. The cones of the skytips were more than ever a lunar fantasy, the bleached and cratered pinnacles of burned-out volcanoes.

"You've farther to go than I have," Peter said.

"That is indeed the truth," his companion agreed. "I've much farther to go."

He laughed, and the silence of the wilderness had a peculiarly distorting effect. The laugh sounded eerie. It had an origin in something malignant.

They had come to a bend in the road. There was enough light to reveal the trees in some detail, plenty of light to disclose the car pulled over on to the grass verge. Peter recognised the battered Austin the instant he turned the corner. He saw the fat man peering from the back seat and the jockey figure of the valet at the wheel. He halted. Involuntarily, he took a step backwards. Then, something hard and tubular jabbed him in the small of the back and pressed him forward.

"Keep moving, chum," the curator said. "And don't do anything to disturb the peace. This is where you get the lift I promised you."

Chapter 13

When they took the high road into the clay country, he knew where he was going. Alfie pulled up just off the track behind the lower, flat-topped mound of the disused clay-pit, and they all got out, Peter under the compulsion of a push from Murrison. They were very casual about it, or very sure that no one would come along.

Alfie led the way across the shaky trestle bridge to the winder-house. Next it was Peter's turn, and as he approached the plank, he had a wild thought of escape. Three paces and a leap, and he would be on top of Alfie. One well-aimed blow would fell that shrimp of a man, and then all would depend on fleetness of foot. With Alfie winded and the fat man useless in a chase, he would have only the curator to outdistance, and he thought he could do it. The way round the rim of the pit was clear. He could skirt the skytip, reach the car, and be off.

Murrison might have a pistol. The curator had none. He had tricked Peter with a box-spanner. In the car he had turned it over and over in one hand just to show what a bright boy he was. Murrison could be a good shot, and there was plenty of light for the purpose. The sun would not be up for some time yet, but the clouds had broken and the moon was making a premature day of it.

Peter weighed the chances in a fraction of time. He knew what was going to happen to him if he didn't escape. The same thing had happened to Braddock.

"What's the trouble, chum?" the curator asked. "Afraid the bridge might break? Get going!"

Here, they were right at the base of the great cone. The tram-tracks and cables of the dumping equipment ran down from the high pinnacle, passed under the bridge, and descended two hundred feet or more. When you looked down, the angle of the incline was terrifying, and a few yards beyond the far end of the bridge, the drop from the rim was sheer. If you were at all nervous of heights, the bridge alone was enough to bring on an attack of vertigo,

Peter wondered if Braddock had gone down that way. The curator was right. He was afraid of the bridge; but it was the least of his fears.

"Grab the rail, chum, and get going!"

There were moon shadows, but the scene looked flat. Under the pale wash of light it had the distorted perspective of a nightmare.

Peter advanced a foot on to the yielding plank. He watched the shadow of the waiting Alfie on the pipe clayed earth. The shadow vanished, and the light dimmed down as a patch of cloud obscured the moon.

That decided him. He leaped forward, making the plank swing with his weight so that the man behind must be checked for a moment. He hurled himself at Alfie, determined to put everything he had into his well-aimed blow. The impetus he developed would certainly have winded Alfie, but Alfie was too quick to be caught like that. Peter rushed on vacancy, and the next instant he was held from behind, helpless and in agony, as Alfie found points of pressure with two hard thumbs. When he was released, he fell forward on to his knees. He blinked, shaking his head. There was a cold whiteness all around him, and he saw that the moon had come out again. The curator was smiling down at him, and the fat man was pointing a pistol.

"Put that damned thing away!" Alfie ordered Murrison. "You made a mess of the last job. This time you keep out of it."

"I only wanted – "

"Shut up! I know what you wanted." The little man was in a fierce mood. "You, Ackland! If you want to save yourself a lot of trouble, you'd better talk. Where's Braddock's letter?"

There was no reason left in Peter. He was trembling with rage. He got slowly to his feet and stared at Alfie.

"Ask Braddock!" he snarled.

"I'm asking you. You know where it's hidden. You didn't take it to London with you, or you wouldn't have doubled back here."

"Braddock said nothing to me. I never saw any letter."

"Is that so?" Alfie came a step nearer to him. "Why did you go to London, then? Why did you see that newspaper man? Why did you go to Britt at the House of Commons?"

"You tell me!"

"Yes, I'll tell you. You cooked up a plan with Braddock. If anything happened to him, you were to follow up the business."

"He made no plan with me. I just wanted to know what had happened to him. That's why I went to London. Anyway, why don't you ask Braddock?" he paused and looked at Murrison. "Or *can't* you ask him any more?"

Alfie turned to the other two. "Bring him inside," he said.

They seized Peter, one on either side, and led him into the winder-house. It was dark. Very little light filtered in. Murrison proceeded to make it darker. He took off his raincoat and hung it over the window. He closed the door. Then he lit a candle and stuck it in the neck of a beer bottle. The fat man wheezed and panted through these simple operations, while Alfie waited. In this private life of theirs, their relationship was reversed. The master was now the servant; the valet, the master.

Peter was finding his rage-deadened senses again. He knew that he was in great danger, and the knowledge seemed to sharpen his awareness of things. He saw the shaking hand that held the match to the candle, but this was only what his eyes took in. He saw that Murrison was almost too frightened to think, and his mind flashed back to the scene in the bar-room on the morning after the departure of Braddock. Murrison and the supposed valet had searched Braddock. That much they had admitted to Jessica Trask. They had brought Braddock to this winder-house, of course and no one had seen him since. Whatever had happened had thrown Murrison off balance, because, the morning after, he had drunk himself into a stupor.

Murrison had made a mess of the last job. . . .

Alfie was savagely hostile, and Alfie was now the master. They had brought Braddock here to make him talk, and they had failed. Murrison had bungled the job. If he had bungled it irreparably, there was only one possible explanation. Braddock was dead.

Alfie said: "You've had a minute to think it over, Ackland. What do you say?"

"I've told you", Peter answered. "If you want information, you'll have to ask Braddock."

He knew that what they had done to Braddock was going to be done to him; except that they would keep him alive till he told them about the cistern. The one hope he had was to tell them nothing. Silence would buy time, and time might bring rescue. If no word came from him, Woodforde Bayles would become curious. The girl, too, would be anxious, if only for Britt. One or other of them might go to the police. There was another hope, with a promise of more immediate action. As soon as it was light, as soon as the sun came up and work started in the active clay-pits, anyone might come this way. Hicks, the pit manager, used the road that skirted the skytip, and might take it into his head to inspect the winder-house. Any motorist taking a short-cut across the clay country to Bosverran might stop to have a look round. The situation was full of fantastic risks for his captors. It was incredible that they should plan to keep him here, yet this must be their intention. Otherwise why had they brought him to the winder-house?

Peter could see only the one purpose in their act. They were going to hold him, and starve or beat him into submission, and it seemed that they were in a hurry to begin on him.

The master of ceremonies ordered him to strip to the waist. When, to gain time, he refused, Murrison and the curator did it for him. Next his arms were piniioned with a strap that Murrison hauled from a pocket. Another held his legs together above the knees; a third was tightened around his ankles. Murrison sweated and fumbled. He was wax-white with fear. He turned to Alfie with a plea that had panic in it.

"Get it over," he begged. "We haven't got much time. Get it over."

Alfie paid no heed. He was up on a chair, passing the end of a strong rope through a ring-bolt in one of the beams. All Peter's calculations were drowned in a sickening wave of horror as he saw the operation. He fought against it, grasping at any argument in the moment of shock. It couldn't be that they were going to put that rope round his neck. He would be no use to them dead. As long as they believed he had Braddock's treasured letter or knew where it was, he was much too valuable a property to be disposed of. Yet the fear in Murrison was the fear of something about to happen. The fat man was doing something under compulsion.

Peter saw that there was no loop or slip-knot in the rope. It was, perhaps, just a stage property, an effect, the symbol of a threat. It was intended to soften him up, to break him down, to play upon his nerves till his will gave way.

He shaped the argument in his mind, but it was the wrong argument. The rope was no trick. It was just a utility piece of hemp, and its purpose was starkly practical. Alfie looped it round the pinioning strap that passed under Peter's shoulders. He tied it securely, then hauled on the free end, and the trussed Peter was lifted. Not very much. Just slightly. The toes of his shoes still touched the floor. Alfie made sure of that before he fastened the rope round an iron cleat.

The position was not too uncomfortable at first. Peter felt a tendency to spin, but he could stop that with his toes. He could also ease the drag of his weight on the hard strap under his shoulders by standing tiptoe. Otherwise he was quite helpless. He might have been a suspended ham. Or a punching bag.

Murrison was shivering like a man with malaria. He took a flask from his hip and drank, and Peter caught a breath of it.

So he was still on the whisky. Shot to pieces and on the whisky.

The curator might have been watching the arrangement of a new case of specimens. He smiled at Peter.

"Better speak up, chum," he advised. "The doctor knows what's good for you."

Alfie was making a wad of lint. It was clean lint.

"Changed your mind?" he asked.

"I tell you I never saw any letter," Peter answered.

"When you change your mind, spread out your fingers like this." Alfie hooked up his hands as if he, too, were suspended. He extended his fingers fanwise in front of his sternum. "Like that," he added, and then, with a quick continuous movement, he produced the gag of lint, forced it into Peter's mouth, and secured it with more lint.

The curator chuckled. He had a fine sense of humour. He hooked up his hands and spread his fingers fanwise.

"I'd think twice, chum," he said. "It mayn't be nice."

It wasn't nice. How long it went on, Peter didn't know. After the first black-out, time was lost to him, and he couldn't tell from the dawn outside, because the window was darkened and the only light in the world was the smoky candle in the neck of the beer bottle. You couldn't tell, either, by the alternating periods of experience and non-experience, because they were peculiarly personal and not calibrated for the measurement of anything, not even the capacity to suffer. Suffering might imply an experience of conventional time, but there were moments when you were sure there was no such thing, because you were quite positive you did not exist. You were dead, as they wanted you to be. But you wouldn't stay dead. You came back instead to the agony of dying.

What Alfie knew about anatomy he knew well. He knew all the bones and muscles and nerve centres. Judo had once been a practice with a high moral tradition, but there were always those who would take such a thing and put it to their own uses. Alfie, it became clear at a later stage, had picked up his knowledge in the Pacific, where he had knocked about as supernumerary in the engine-rooms of Chinese-owned tramps. Alfie liked engines and machines. He'd driven an electric tram in Sydney and worked a generating plant in San Francisco. In many ways Alfie was a very capable little man.

His thumbs shifted over his victim's thighs, found two points, and pressed.

That was the first time Peter spread his fingers.

Whether he had meant to be or not, he was defiant again by the time the gag was out of his mouth.

Now he lied and kept repeating the lie. He knew the technique of

Murrison and his friends. Say the same lie over and over again and it would become the truth. That was the line to take. He must convince these people that his lie was the truth.

"I don't know where the letter is. I know nothing about it."

Murrison was up on the driving platform, sitting on the motorman's bench. Even from this distance you could see the sweat on his forehead. You could see the shivering that raked his fat body. He was a sick man. Sick with fear.

"Nothing, nothing, nothing!" Peter shouted. "I know nothing about the letter. I never met Braddock till I came down here. Ask Murrison. He believes me. Murrison! You believe me, Murrison!"

It wasn't calculated. It wasn't even a chance shot. He was just flailing round, no longer capable of deliberate effort. A thought, if you could call it a thought, became an obsession for a moment.

"Murrison! Murris – "

The gag was in his mouth again, and the little man was reciting the case against him in a tone of surly indifference, as if he didn't care, as if this whole business were something that just had to be got through.

"When you came down here, you made straight for Braddock's house. When something happened to him, you went to London and tried to see Britt. You did everything that Braddock would have done. You talked to the *Gazette* man. You took him along with you to see Jessica Trask. Why he went with you, I don't know, but you shook him off. Then you went to the House of Commons with the girl. You made a deal with Britt and came back here to get the letter. And before I've done with you, you'll tell me where it is."

Peter spread his fingers, but his eyes must have shown that he would do no more than repeat the lie. The little man shook his head and moved forward again. He was vicious, but he took no pleasure in this business He had not the sadistic cat-throwing cruelty of the fat asthmatic, and that was the peculiar contradiction in the set-up. Murrison should be enjoying the scene, yearning to do the job himself. Instead, he was remote in his sick fear; not even watching.

It began again, and Peter closed his eyes. And now the gag was the worst thing. It became an obsession. He must get rid of the gag, or it would kill him. He would choke, or something inside him would be torn apart. He could stand no more of it. He was beaten ready to surrender. He would tell them anything they wanted to know, if only they would let him scream.

He gave the signal with his fingers, but, when the lint was removed from his mouth, he could not scream. No sound would come. He felt a hand touch him, to stay the swing of his body. He heard the inevitable question about the letter. He tried to speak, but he had forgotten how. He had a sensation of spinning madly, of falling into darkness.

The next thing he knew he was lying on the floor. The straps had been removed, and he was dressed again in shirt and pullover and jacket. He had a marvellous feeling of peace and ease, as if his hurts had been miraculously cured. Marvellous. The word came to him over and over in the daze between sleep and wakefulness. He had to struggle to a perception of his own position. Then he snapped into consciousness, and there followed a period of mental clarity.

It came quite suddenly. It was like a curtain going up on a scene in full action, but it was no remote piece of play-acting. He was closely involved; the spring and purpose of the scene. Murrison and Alfie were in the middle of a bitter quarrel.

"You can go on till doomsday," Murrison was saying. "If the man doesn't know where the letter is how can he tell you?"

"He knows," Alfie insisted. "It's plain that he knows."

"You stubborn fool. I tell you he was a stranger to Braddock. You're so suspicious of everybody, you can never see a simple truth. If you go on with this farce, what happens? He tells you any old lie, and you believe him. You can't check, because you can't hold him. We've got to finish this business and get out. Do you want to stay here till they catch you? Do you want us all to swing for Braddock?"

"No! Only you!" The little man was all venom.

The curator intervened. "Listen, Alfie! Nat's right. We've got to cut our losses and get out. I don't think this fellow does know where the letter is, but he knows too much, and we can't turn him loose."

"He knows more than we do," Alfie insisted.

"Then you should have grabbed him before he went to London," Murrison said quickly. "I left you here to clean things up, and you bungled everything."

"I bungled?" Alfie was at the highest peak of fury. "I suppose *I* did in Braddock?"

"For God's sake!" Murrison's anger was swamped by a tidal wave of fear and self-pity. "You know it was an accident. It was your fault as much as mine. *You* tied the rope round his neck. I – I was just trying to make him talk."

"That's good! There's the master mind for you! Hear that, Keutel! If you want to make a man talk, you lose your temper, pull on a rope, and throttle him! Look at him? Look at the great man! He's seeing Braddock's ghost. He didn't want to come here again. He's shaking in his boots. The mountain's shaking. He's afraid Braddock will come walking down that clay dump out there. Look at him!"

"Okay, look at him," the curator agreed. "Take a look at yourself, too. We've got to cut and run. It's getting light outside and we haven't much time. You've had your go at Ackland. What are you going to do with him?"

Murrison promptly answered the question with another. "Put him in a truck and shoot him over the top of the dump? That's splendid!"

Alfie resented the tone of criticism. "Nobody's found Braddock," he snapped in self-defence. "Nobody will find him in a hundred years."

"Don't these clay people notice when a truck has been moved?" the curator asked.

"The trucks are just as they were." Alfie was impatient. "There's been nothing to notice – so far."

"What about the noise?"

"When you've got that noise going on all day, you don't pay any attention."

The student of *The Psychology of Reasoning* wasn't satisfied with the argument. "You do if you hear it at the wrong hour," he objected.

"That's what I keep telling him," Murrison complained. "The last time it was all right. There was a storm on. There's no storm this morning. He's mad."

"Mad, is it!" Alfie's voice leaped in pitch. "You . . ."

The curator interposed. "Maybe he's right, Alfie. I don't know how much noise the thing makes – "

"None at all," Alfie cut in. "Nothing to worry about. I'll show you. Go to the door and watch. I'm going to bring the truck up from the pit. Tell me when it reaches the foot-bridge. That's where we want it. Right under the foot-bridge."

Peter heard the clunk of the circuit-maker being thrown. He wanted to see what was going on, but his first slight movement caused him such a stab of pain, he gave up the idea. He became aware of a dim light from outside when the curator opened the door. He heard the whine of the motor, the metallic tap as the clutch was operated. The great winding drum began to move with a low rumbling sound. There was little noise from the pit. The wagon was coming up slowly, very slowly, with a minimum of sound. It would wait under the swaying footbridge for a passenger.

He marvelled that he did not panic at once and leap for the door in an effort to escape. It was, perhaps, panic that held him immovable while his mind fled frantically from the thought of death to the thought that death must be avoided. If he kept his wits about him he might find some way out. He must listen carefully to everything that was said. It was important to understand everything, vitally important, and he was puzzled now by Alfie's claim that there had been no change in the position of the wagons after Braddock's ride up the incline. In the customary order there were two wagons on the twin tracks, one going up, the other descending; one full of rock and rubble, the other empty. If there had been no change, the empty wagon must have been brought down from the skytip and sent up again with Braddock. Then Alfie had climbed to the top on that night of storm to dispose of Braddock.

But this time he was going to use the loaded wagon from the floor of the pit. There would be no need for him to go to the top after it, because at the end of the uptrack there was a device that tripped a lever on the side of the wagon and automatically discharged the burden. Everything that the wagon carried would go tumbling down the flank of the great cone to pile up in a broken heap on the flat top of the lower mound.

Everything the wagon carried at the moment the trap flew open. That was the important reservation, the vital point to hold in mind.

If he could keep his wits about him. . . .

The man he still thought of as the curator spoke from the doorway of the throbbing winder-house.

"Here she comes. Go easy."

Now you could hear in slow rhythm the whispering clack of wheels over track joints.

Clack . . . clack . . . clack. . . .

"Easy. Go easy. Stop."

The motor died on an expiring whine. Cooling metal whimpered and there was a smell of hot oil. A smell and an oily vapour . . . a haze.

He feared the haze. He must fight against it, keep his head.

The curator came inside and closed the door. "Okay," he said. "She's right under the bridge. Let's get . . ."

Hearing was difficult. The haze was thickening. It was like the swirl of last night's fog in Old Palace Yard. The trio were arguing again. The voices faded, came back, faded. They issued from behind the statue of Coeur de Lion. The curator wanted more details. It was made clear to him that the plan was thorough, perfect. The body would go plunging down to the lower mound, and Alfie would climb up to make sure. Make sure it was covered, make sure, make sure, make sure. . . .

Thought oscillated. Images, hopes, fears spun in confusion, and it was impossible to sort them out with all the hammering din of the division bells.

Suddenly the bells stopped and everything was clear again. Too clear.

"Ackland!"

It was Murrison's voice.

Chapter 14

HE gave no sign that he had heard. He remained still, facing the fact that his effort to gain time had been futile, because the end had been determined before the beginning. They had brought him here to kill him because he was a witness they feared. They believed they would be safe when he was removed. They would go on in the belief that nobody else could suspect them.

Another swirl of fog enveloped him. The miraculous cure of his hurts had been an illusion, a kind of anaesthesia that had passed. Bruised nerve ends throbbed all over his body. He strove to clear his mind. He had to think; to find and hold on to the last small hope.

If he were alive and conscious when they put him in the wagon, he would have a chance. If not, he must face at least three hazards. He might be caught by the shark's snap of the discharging trap, he might break his neck in the initial fall from the wagon, he might be crushed by debris in the plunge down the mound.

The hope was that he would be conscious and have enough strength left to leap from the wagon before it reached the tipping point. If he blacked out, if he could not rouse himself when the journey started up the incline, then he was finished.

It was unlikely they would truss him up again. Straps could be evidence; might be traced. Alfie would leave things as tidy as possible, Alfie kept an eye on the realities. The wagon must carry dead weight.

Peter knew what he must do. He must persuade his captors that he was unconscious and resist any efforts they might make to restore him. Whatever they did to him, he must show no sign of life. At any cost.

Murrison came across the floor and bent down in the corner near the door. Peter was as sure of it as if he had his eyes open, watching the man. The sound picture was unmistakable: the ponderous, waddling tread; the distressed grunt.

"Here's his coat," Murrison said. "We'd better get that on him, too. We don't want to leave anything around."

Peter heard urgency in the wheezing voice. He took hope that his deception would be easy; that they intended to be rid of him at once.

The hope had a very short life.

"Wait a minute!" Alfie's tone was scathing as well as peremptory. "I haven't finished with him."

The plunge back into fear was destructive. Resistance would now be instinctive, with little will to support it.

Peter heard light footsteps near his head. Alfie's fingers grasped his chin and swung it to one side, then to the other. Peter knew the scrutiny was close. When the man's hand came down sharply across his face, he still gave no sign of feeling. Then the firm, sensitive fingers were on his right thumb, feeling for the joint at the metacarpal bone. He knew what was coming. He wanted to scream, to use all his breath in screaming before the wad of lint added to the torture. He struggled to be silent, but the struggle was obvious and at last he cried out in pain.

The little man dragged him up by the armpits, stood him reeling on his feet, struck him twice across the face, sending him back against the motorman's platform. He didn't follow up. He stood staring at Peter across two yards of space. There was no more of the cold deliberation about him. He was ready to pounce in anger.

"You want more of it, do you?" he asked.

He could read everything in Peter's mind except the one thing that he most desired to know.

"Are you going to answer?" he demanded. "Do you want more of it?"

"No, no." Peter leaned back, supporting himself with his hands grasping the edge of the platform. He found that he was acting still. He could have stood without support. Hope surged up again.

"All right. Where did Braddock hide the letter?"

'I'll tell you. Give me time. Give me a drink." A flash had come to him, a delayed spark from the talk he had overheard. Under pressure he might tell any lie, and they couldn't check it unless they held him. He wanted a second, a split-second, to think about it. There was a way he could use a lie. He could buy time with a lie – an hour or two hours or even a day. If only he could think of a feasible place for the letter.

"Give him your flask," Alfie ordered Murrison.

Peter took a mouthful of whisky.

"I'll tell you," he said. "Braddock hid the letter in the skytip near his house."

"In that rubble?" Alfie was sceptical.

"Yes. He buried it. He thought no one would think of looking for it outside." Peter tried urgently to counter the man's disbelief with persuasive detail. "He put it in an old tin and buried it."

"Where did he bury it?"

Disbelief had been reduced to doubt. Peter rushed on into more detail. "On the side facing Bosverran. There's a big boulder in the field, near the edge of the road. You take a line with a smaller boulder and climb the mound – about five yards up. I can't explain. I'll have to show you."

Alfie swung back to disbelief. "You'll have to explain," he said.

"It's under a stone. Queer shape." Peter motioned with his hands. "I'll show you if you'll take me there."

"That would be nice, wouldn't it? That would be quite an outing for you."

The man was watching him intently. Peter's voice rose in desperation. "But you'll never find it unless I go with you," he shouted. "You can go on till doomsday."

Till doomsday! The instant that echo of Murrison's phrase was out, he realised its fatal implication. To the suspicious mind it was as good as saying that he had overheard Murrison's argument; had taken a hint from it and invented this fiction.

Alfie leapt at him, striking. Peter struck back and landed a blow that swept the smaller man aside. He saw the way clear to the door and took it in a despairing attempt to get out. He grasped the handle but had no time to turn it. A blow on the back of the head swung him away from the door and, before he could make a defensive movement, the curator's fist crashed on his jaw.

There were vague patches of consciousness, like whorls of dim light in a very black night. In one patch he was being carried. In another he was dumped down on the planks of the trestle bridge. He struggled to open his eyes for a moment. The faint light of the grey dawn penetrated his darkness and he saw the steep incline of the tram-tracks against the clay white dust. He saw the wagon beneath him with its load of rubble from the deep pit. His body was bent and his arms hung down towards the wagon, reaching. He was sliding from the plank, back into the night.

It seemed a long time, a very long time. Then he heard the grinding of wheels on rails and the clack-clack as they went over the joints. He had a sense of movement. The clacking was going on under him, in slow rhythm.

Clack-clack . . . clack-clack . . .

Suddenly his head cleared. He struggled, but something impeded movement. Effort was agony, but he must use all his strength. He had the hoped-for chance if he could realise it. Something was gripping his arm, pressing into his flesh with hard fingers.

Clack-clack . . . clack-clack . . . the speed of the wheels slowly increased.

He was going up towards the sky.

His right arm came free and he was able to raise his clattering head a little. He saw the blanket of stones they had piled on him. He saw the earth gliding away from him, the deep pit and the powdered fields. The trestle bridge was far away and slowly sinking.

He tugged at the stones with his free hand, but the pain was too much to be endured. Something had gone wrong with his right hand. He got his left hand clear and pushed and tugged at the stones. Some fell away and went bounding down the track. He worked frantically, aware of the steady progress upward, up towards the projecting structure where the rails ended.

Clack-clack. . . .

The end of the journey was in the sky. There the trap below him would open and he would be pitched down. Unless the closing jaws caught him first and mangled him.

He twisted and strained to get his body free. He sat up and bending over tore at the rock. It didn't matter about his right hand now. At least the fingers were good, and he must suffer the pain of the thumb.

The wagon had passed the level of the lower, flat-topped mound. He could look over the plateau, weather-worn and strewn with fragments of granite. He could look out over all the clay country. He thought he saw a car coming along the Liskeard road, taking the short cut to Bosverran. It was a car, because a few seconds later he heard the sound of a horn, very near.

The thought flashed upon him that it could be the skipper of works, but Hicks, if it were Hicks, would never reach the winder-house in time.

No one could help him. What he could not do himself, would never be done. He bedded his hands firmly on the sharp pointed rubble and heaved.

Clack-clack, clack-clack, clack-clack.

From the slow crawl, the ascent had become an urgent soaring. The wheels screamed on the rails, the cable slapped on the sleepers. For some reason the man on the driving platform had swung the control to full speed.

The rubble moved and shifted over Peter's legs. He flexed his left knee, and heaved again. He was free. He turned to get on his knees. The wagon was rushing upward, the end of the rails frighteningly close. He raised himself and stood drunkenly for a moment on the swaying load. He heard a sharp crack from far below. It sounded like a shot from a pistol, but, if a bullet had been aimed at him, it had missed. The thought of a new threat spurred him to the final effort. He braced himself for an instant and then jumped wildly.

He hit the rubble with his heels, and white dust spurted. Above the wagon crashed and clanged and sent its small avalanche down the flank of the cone, but by that time he was rolling down the slope at a safe distance, clawing, digging in his heels, sliding, tumbling, sliding again, until he reached the flat top of the lower mound.

He lay for a moment, breathless, but a moment was all he could spare. They would be climbing to the plateau after him, for he was sure they had seen him leap from the skip. He must cross the mound to the far side and get down to the roadway. It was light now and there was a chance of finding help, a clay-worker on a bike, a car. One car had passed. Another car. . . .

The sound of an engine starting up reached him. It revved dizzily. Then the car took the clutch and darted off somewhere.

A shout, a loud shout. Silence.

He was on his feet, staggering over the weather-packed surface of the mound. His face was gashed and blood was running from a torn hand. He took no notice. He felt that all his body was torn and bleeding. Part of his ripped coat flapped round his ankles as he went on. He saw with dazed vision a bulk of granite in his way, but he had no strength to swerve and avoid it. He stumbled, lurched, went down. In the silence a sound of coughing came up from below, the choking, asthmatic cough of the fat-man, followed by the whining, gasping noises he made in his agony.

Murrison was there, on the ground level by the winder-house.

Peter rose again, and he still had strength to go on. He came near to the edge, very near. He heard a rattle of rubble falling, dislodged by a climber. He gave up. He had no more strength. One of them had anticipated his move and had come up from the road-side.

He went down on his knees to ease the pain in his legs. Except for the one clear fact of the unseen climber, there was confusion in his head. So much confusion, so much he couldn't understand. The engine starting up, the car speeding off, Murrison in his asthmatic paroxysm. It didn't make sense, because he was sure the engine he had heard belonged to the battered Austin.

Sense or no sense, he was finished. He might try a last desperate throw with the climber, but he knew it would soon be over. He might hurl a piece of sharp granite, but he could not trust his left-hand aim and his right hand was useless.

His fingers closed on a fragment of rock, and again he got up on his feet. He lurched forward a step, and teetered back. He saw a head and shoulders rise above the edge of the mound, and he dropped his missile.

The climber was Jessica Trask.

Chapter 15

HER story came to him in bits and pieces, and he found it difficult at first to arrange them in the right order. Pain, shock, exhaustion and the sedatives they gave him in the Bosverran Hospital dulled his perceptions. Even when the worst of his ills had receded and the hospital was prepared to let him go, it was an effort to think clearly about what had happened. Some things had to be repeated.

Soon after she had telephoned Bayles from Paddington, they had set out by car with the object of reaching him before he got to Braddock's house. They had hoped to intercept him at Bosverran Road, but the fog round London had deprived them of the advantage they might have gained from the train's taking the long route by way of Bristol.

"So we took the shortest cut to Bosverran," she had said. "That's how we came to see *their* car."

"The Austin?"

"Yes. As soon as I told him about it, Jim made our driver pull up, and they went to investigate. Then I saw you fall from that wagon, and climbed up to you."

"What happened down there?"

"Alfie and another man got in the Austin and drove off."

"Not Murrison?"

"No. I told you."

Once again he could not remember what had happened to Murrison. "What made you come rushing down here?" he had asked.

"It was Jim. When I 'phoned him, I told him what had happened.

He was worried about your being watched by that man at the House. I told him that Murrison was down here, and he thought you were running into danger. That's why he stopped when I told him that the Austin was Alfie's car."

He wasn't interested in Jim Bayles any more. He was thinking bitterly that his own request to her to telephone Bayles had brought the two of them together. The quarrel had been forgotten.

"I was such a fool," she had said. "I shouldn't have let you come down here alone. I might have seen the danger. I saw it quickly enough when Jim pointed it out."

Jim again! Then he had remembered about Murrison.

Bayles and the driver of the hired car had tackled the trio in the winder-house. The attempt of Bayles to delay Murrison and his companions until they had explained themselves had led to a struggle. Alfie and the curator had made a break for it while Murrison covered their retreat by holding the trestle bridge with his revolver. It had looked like a complete check for Bayles and the driver, but at the critical moment of his own retreat, Murrison had started wheezing and gasping. Bayles had rushed him, and a wild shot had gone harmlessly into the wall of the winder-house. After that, Murrison had hung helplessly to the handrail of the bridge, deserted by the valet with his ephedrine, dependent on his captors for first-aid.

The fit had been a bad one, and he had had to be carried into the Bosverran police station a few minutes later. Peter had wanted to stay with Bayles, to supply his own description of the fugitives in the Austin, but Jessica Trask had insisted on rushing him to hospital.

He remembered that; remembered, too, how curious he had found it that she should be so concerned about a dislocated thumb when she had not turned a hair over the danger faced by Bayles from the pistol of the fat Horatius. She had been very gentle, he remembered, and the memory brought with it a curious pang.

Well, he would see her for the last time in another hour when she called with Bayles to take him from the hospital to Braddock's house. It seemed that she and Bayles had decided between them that the fate of Britt's letter must be left to his judgment, since he was the only person who knew where to find it.

He thought that was very kind of them. Very kind . . . Did she perhaps think that he would give her the letter, that Britt could be safe after all?

He paced the floor to the window and back again to the bed. He stared along the road from Bosverran at every turn. When they were late, he became anxious. The car came at last, and she was alone with the chauffeur.

"Are you feeling better?" she asked.

"There's nothing wrong with me," he said curtly.

She smiled. There was some sort of secret satisfaction in her smile. She was sure of herself. She knew he would give her the letter. He felt almost sorry for the wretched Bayles.

"Jim's going to meet us at the house," she said. "He's waiting to get another call through to London. There's news, by the way. The police have picked up Alfie. It was just outside Southampton. The other man was wise enough to leave the car, but not Alfie. That car was like a god to him. He would never have abandoned it."

There could be no question about the loveliness of her eyes.

"What did you say about the car?" he asked.

She repeated it.

It was the sort of thing you might expect from men like Alfie and Murrison. Shambling, incompetent, treacherous. When they wanted to keep a man alive, they murdered him. When they tried to murder, they failed. It was no wonder that the curator had skipped off on his own. He had a little self-respect. One could almost admire him. One could be sure he would make an effective disappearance.

"I almost forgot to tell you" she said. "They've found Braddock's body. It was on that lower mound, covered over with rubble."

They waited in the garden of Braddock's house till Bayles arrived, then Peter opened the door and led the way to the bathroom.

The table from the landing stood under the manhole and the trap had been thrown back. Alfie had returned; Murrison too, perhaps. They had come very near to the hiding-place, but they had not thought of looking for a letter under the water.

Bayles expressed incredulity when Peter told him to climb up and look in the cistern.

Peter insisted. "You'll find it in some sort of canister."

There was a moment when doubt came to him. Bayles bared an arm and fished in the water. He was a long time about it, but at last he found the blind-cord and hauled up a cocoa-tin. The lid had been soldered on clumsily, and solder had been splashed along the joints.

They took the find down to the kitchen, and a few taps from a hammer caused the feebly-sealed lid to spring open. The contents were several pieces of battered lead and an envelope.

Peter tore the flap of the envelope and removed two sheets of paper. One was a note on official German stationery according credentials to Major John Prester-John for propaganda work among British prisoners-of-war. The other was a handwritten letter to the Commandant of a prisoner-of-war camp in the Rhineland.

Peter's German was weak, but he could make out that the letter had something to do with facilities to be granted to the signatory, John Prester-John. And he could clearly understand the inscription printed in block letters across the top of the sheet. The Herr Kommandant was enjoined to destroy when read. The Herr Kommandant had been neglectful.

Bayles and Jessica Trask were watching him intently when he looked up. Peter passed the second letter to the girl.

"Is it Britt's handwriting?" he asked.

"Yes." Her lips trembled.

Peter looked through the window at the great skytip that obscured the view. "Do you understand German?"

"Not very well."

The skytip was very white in the sun. High up in the blue above the cone a white bird was flying.

"He's explaining to the commandant that he has to interview British prisoners." He handed her the other sheet. "This is a sort of introduction. It says that Major Prester-John has been successful in getting British recruits for the Free Corps to fight against the Russians."

If the bird was a gull, it was a long way from the sea. Or perhaps this wasn't far from the sea in gull mileage. There was some superstition about gulls that flew inland, but he couldn't remember what it was.

He said: "These letters are not my responsibility. I give them to you. That's what you've wanted me to do, isn't it?"

She was silent. She walked to the window and handed the letters to Bayles.

"I'm sorry, Jim," she said.

Bayles put his hand on her shoulder and gave it a squeeze. It was an avuncular sort of gesture, or paternal. It certainly wasn't a lover's caress.

"We may not have to use this stuff, Jess," he said. "It looks as if we've won the fight without it. I heard the news when I 'phoned the office just now. I didn't want to tell you till you'd seen the evidence. Britt skipped out last night, by air. Apparently he'd been making plans for some weeks. There's a rumour he's landed in Portugal, but the general idea seems to be that he's beating it to South America."

She took it as if it didn't matter.

"I must start back now, Jess," Bayles told her. "You keep out of it down here for a few days, and then come to our place. Mary and I will be glad to have you."

Why should he, Peter Ackland, feel suddenly as if a mine had exploded under him? It didn't mean anything to him if Jim Bayles was married.

"Good-bye, Ackland. Sorry I can't stop, but I must get that car back to town. Look me up when you return."

He shook hands, patted the girl, and urged her to cheer up. He went out quickly and the door slammed behind him, and then the girl said she had to find a mirror because she couldn't go out looking like this.

Peter waited for her, waited to lock up the house. She smiled faintly at him and her eyes were at their loveliest, but in a moment there would be no more of her. Whatever little regrets he might feel, the adventure was over, except for the final farewell.

They walked down the hall with its litter of papers, and she waited while he made sure that the door was fast, and then they went together to the garden gate. It was all very much as it had been on that other day, only this time there was the ruthlessness of an ending about it.

"You've been very good to me, Mr. Ackland," she said. "I'll never forget your kindness."

He felt hurt. This wasn't right somehow.

"There's nothing to forget," he said, and that didn't sound right at all. In fact, it was so hopelessly wrong that he became confused, and the scar on his cheek felt like a hot wire. "Will you be going back to the same house in Bosverran?" he asked. Anything to cover his confusion.

"Yes." She could even laugh now. "I've got a week's room-rent to work off. I brought some things back in case of need, so I might as well stay. There's nothing for me in London now."

Caution had to be thrown away, if only for the sake of decency.

"Well," he said. "Perhaps you'd like to come to the farm to tea tomorrow. Would you?"

"That would be nice," she told him.

When she had gone, he turned at the gate and looked over the neglected garden, and up at the dripless waste pipe, and back at the porch. He saw the figure of Braddock in the doorway, teetering on pigeon-toes, holding his hands before him as if he were about to push his way through a jungle.

He closed his eyes, and when he opened them there were only the empty doorway and the deserted unkempt garden. He felt intolerably lonely then, and a wilderness of time stretched between now and the tea-hour tomorrow.

The girl was going slowly along the road, back to Bosverran, and there was something about her walk that told him her desolation was greater than his.

Tomorrow, he had said, and there was all the rest of to-day to get through, and to-night. It was intolerable. Surely there came a time when even an emotional bankrupt was entitled to apply for his discharge.

He hurried after her, knowing that this time there would be no battered Austin waiting for her round the other side of the gleaming

skytip.
"Jessica!" he called. "Oh, Jessica!"

Eric Ambler

Doctor Frigo ISBN: 978-07551-2381-0
A coup d'etat in a Caribbean state causes a political storm in the region and even the seemingly impassive and impersonal Doctor Castillo, nicknamed Doctor Frigo, cannot escape the consequences. As things heat up, Frigo finds that both his profession and life are horribly at risk.

'As subtle, clever and complex as always' - Sunday Telegraph

'The book is a triumph' - Sunday Times

Judgment on Deltchev ISBN: 978-07551-1762-8
Foster is hired to cover the trial of Deltchev, who is accused of treason for allegedly being a member of the sinister and secretive Brotherhood and preparing a plot to assassinate the head of state whilst President of the Agrarian Socialist Party and member of the Provisional Government. It is assumed to be a show trial, but when Foster encounters Madame Deltchev the plot thickens, with his and other lives in danger ....

'The maestro is back again, with all his sinister magic intact' - The New York Times

The Maras Affair ISBN: 978-07551-1764-2
(Ambler originally writing as Eliot Reed with Charles Rodda)
Charles Burton, journalist, cannot get work past Iron Curtain censors and knows he should leave the country. However, he is in love with his secretary, Anna Maras, and she is in danger. Then the President is assassinated and one of Burton's office workers is found dead. He decides to smuggle Anna out of the country, but her reluctance impedes him, as does being sought by secret police and counter-revolutionaries alike.

Eric Ambler

The Schirmer Inheritance   ISBN: 978-07551-1765-9
Former bomber pilot George Carey becomes a lawyer and his first job with a Philadelphia firm looks tedious - he is asked to read through a large quantity of files to ensure nothing has been missed in an inheritance case where there is no traceable heir. His discoveries, however, lead to unforeseen adventures and real danger in post war Greece.

'Ambler towers over most of his newer imitators' - Los Angeles Times

'Ambler may well be the best writer of suspense stories .. He is the master craftsman' - Life

Topkapi (The Light of Day)   ISBN: 978-07551-1768-0
Arthur Simpson is a petty thief who is discovered stealing from a hotel room. His victim, however, turns out to be a criminal in a league well above his own and Simpson is blackmailed into smuggling arms into Turkey for use in a major jewel robbery. The Turkish police, however, discover the arms and he is further 'blackmailed' by them into spying on the 'gang' - or must rot in a Turkish jail. However, agreeing to help brings even greater danger ....

'Ambler is incapable of writing a dull paragraph' - The Sunday Times

Eric Ambler

Siege at the Villa Lipp (Send No More Roses)
ISBN: 978-07551-1766-6

Professor Krom believes Paul Firman, alias Oberholzer, is one of those criminals who keep a low profile and are just too clever to get caught. Firman, rich and somewhat shady, agrees to be interviewed in his villa on the French Riviera. But events take an unexpected turn and perhaps there is even someone else artfully hiding in the deep background?

'One of Ambler's most ambitious and best' - The Observer

'Ambler has done it again ... deliciously plausible' - The Guardian

The Levanter
ISBN: 978-07551-1941-7

Michael Howell lives the good life in Syria, just three years after the six day war. He has several highly profitable business interests and an Italian office manager who is also his mistress. However, the discovery that his factories are being used as a base by the Palestine Action Force changes everything - he is in extreme danger with nowhere to run ...

'The foremost thriller writer of our time' - Sunday Times

'Our greatest thriller writer' - Graham Greene